Two Boys and a Cage

Andrea Forwood Gregson

First published by Busybird Publishing 2018

ISBN 978-1-925585-72-8

This is a work of fiction. Any similarities between places and characters are a coincidence.

Cover design: Busybird Publishing
Layout and typesetting: Busybird Publishing

Busybird Publishing
2/118 Para Road
Montmorency, Victoria
Australia 3094
www.busybird.com.au

Dedication

I dedicate this book to Katie and Zoey
who are the very best daughter and
granddaughter that I could ever have
been blessed to call my own.

Acknowledgements

T hank you to Mary who ran a writers group that I was privileged to be a member of while living in Hobart.

My thanks also to a very good friend, Margaret, who was also my doctor for many years.

Thanks also to Katie who has been my sounding board and my rock to keep my life in running order.

The towns, places in this book are a work of total fiction and the characters are purely imaginary.

Chapter 1

The classroom was usually quiet and orderly with students gathered together in their own small groups. The only one who seemed always to be caught on the outside was the class loner, Liam. Mrs Brown and other teachers at the school had tried to encourage harmony between all the students. Most of the teachers liked to gather together in the staff-room before classes began, but not Di Brown. She found early mornings were hard for Liam, as the other pupils shunned him and spoke of pleasant things that had happened in their families during the weekend or just the night before. This morning it was hard to judge which outburst was first, the school bell or Liam.

'How old are ya?'

'What's ya name?'

'Why do ya have that thing round ya legs?'

'Come on, ya ain't dumb are ya?'

'Hey, don't push. Mrs Brown, this new kid 'ere was mean ta me.'

'Excuse me, Liam, who was being mean to whom?'

'Well, anyway, what's 'is name, what do we call 'im?'

'Liam, as the bell has gone I was, if you give me some time, just about to introduce our new pupil. Class, as you've already heard from Liam's out-burst we have a new pupil with us. His name is Dylan, Dylan Hunter, and he's here to stay with his grandparents while he attends treatment at the hospital. Perhaps, Dylan, could you tell us a bit about yourself?'

'Er ... yes, Mrs Brown, but what do I have to say?'

'Nothing much. Maybe what your other school is like and how life is different living on a cattle station.'

'Aw come on, what's wrong with 'im, Mrs Brown? Is it somefing I might catch? If so, I'll need to go home and tell me mam. RIGHT NOW.'

'Sit down, Liam, you are a disgrace. Look how you've embarrassed Dylan.'

'Geezzzzz, Mrs Brown.'

'Sit down, Liam. NOW.'

'Mrs Brown, I'll tell the class. I really don't mind, I suppose I'd want to know if I suddenly heard of some new kid in my school. But then it's all so strange because this is the first time I've ever been in a real classroom with lots of desks and chairs and all.'

'Liar. Mrs Brown, he's lying isn't he? 'Cause all schools have classrooms. Liar, liar pants on fire, ya in for it now.'

In hindsight, Mrs Brown now severely chastised herself. With the problems Liam had, she should have known that something different would have set his mind and mouth off at the speed of light.

'No, Liam, he is not making up stories.'

'But, Mrs Brown, all schools 'ave classrooms, even I'm not dumb enough ta know that what Dylan said just ain't true. I've seen a lot of schools and they're all the same.'

'Liam, please. Sometimes I wonder if you are the only pupil in the class. Now, come and use some of that built up energy you've saved up this morning by helping me to move the TV and video stand.'

'Are we going to watch a video, are we, are we? 'Ope it's space invaders, is it?'

With the full weight of exasperation cloaking her, she addressed the rest of the class. 'I was thinking last night that maybe some of you would wonder about the school Dylan has mentioned, so I've borrowed a short video called "School of the Air".'

'Aw, come on, Mrs Brown, air don't need ta go to school, it just knows how and when to blow. Me dad says, "Always see which way the wind's blowing before going out on a job".'

'That's enough, Liam. If you can't be quiet whilst the class watch this, you'll need to spend the period in our time-out area, okay?'

To Mrs Brown's amazement, the boy not only sat quietly once the video had started, but he genuinely looked as though he was taking some interest in how children of isolated areas obtain schooling right in their own homes.

In the short reprieve from full-on Liam, Mrs Brown continued reading the supplied history on Dylan. Mrs Hunter, Dylan's mum, sounded like the kind of mother any young boy would worship. If only Liam had had a chance at family life like this, instead of how his family was forced to live on the tenth floor of a hideous concrete monster that devoured innocent minds and bodies and spewed out delinquent robots. Dylan's mum was not what you would call a super-mum. No, just an old-fashioned thinking person who believed parents should devote their undivided attention to their children's younger years. But then who else was there to demand her time? Only the flying doctor, his nurse and all the wandering patients who called once each month for the local clinic. Then, twice a year, Ted Smith would arrive with his gang of shearers who usually stayed about ten days at a time, but thankfully they had their own cook and generally looked after themselves. The muster-gang, plus horses, at times when the brumbies needed rounding up. Now, they were a rowdy bunch, always up to hijinks of some sort. Then we can't forget the machinery salesman; ever hopeful that the year has been a good one, he then hopes to have a chance at spiriting the properties' hard earned dollars away by updating a tractor or implement. *Deary me, I nearly forgot all the drifters looking for a bed and a meal in exchange for a day's work.* Mrs Hunter was also a stand-in vet, doctor, nurse, counsellor, teacher, accountant, chef and, somewhere squeezed into this collection of titles, a very loving wife and partner. Mrs Brown didn't like to compare parents, but the contrast between the two boys' mothers was like comparing chalk to cheese. Mrs Sims drew attention every time she appeared to the school. Requesting visits by the staff, or demanding ones, when her 'darlings' went home with tales of harassment. In fact, parent/teacher nights were always a nightmare. Mrs Brown knew from personal experience how hard it was to lose just a couple of kilos once a body is past the magical fifties, but standing beside Mrs Sims she imagined herself as a 'prison-camp' refugee. The poor woman was very large indeed. When the headmaster first saw Mrs Sims, his immediate thought was, 'How will my budget stretch for reinforced floors?' Mrs Brown had to say how cruel she thought that comment was during the staff meeting following parent/teacher week. Everyone has the right to be accepted as they are. Unfortunately, it was not only her size that was off-putting, but her manner and occasional use of foul language that usually upset people she came into contact with. Mrs Brown really thought she had made a little headway one year, because at Mrs Sims' next appearance at school, she actually appeared nicely dressed and of cheerful disposition. But alas no; Liam broadcast to the whole class how his mum and dad had a great party, celebrating a small lotto win and they all got something new. In a moment of compassion, Mrs Brown thought again about Liam's mum. She must have been young and energetic once, but to see the size she is now it was quite hard to make your mind visualise a younger, smaller Mrs Sims.

'Mrs Brown. Hey, Mrs Brown.'

Glorious peace was now broken by Liam's raucous voice, that thirty minutes certainly whizzed past quickly.

'Yes, Liam.'

'Do those country hicks—'

'Liam.'

'Sorry, Mrs Brown. Do them country kids really stay home and never go to school?'

'Liam, were you paying any attention to what you and the rest of the class have just been watching on that video?'

'Yeah well, it weren't as good as *Robo Cop*; I watched that last night. But Dylan is the one who said he's never been ta school, didn't he.'

'No, I did not.'

'Did to.'

'Enough, Liam. If you could be quiet and behave yourself for a moment, perhaps Dylan will tell us how he does his lessons with School of the Air.'

'Yeah liar, how's the air school?'

'Liam, I'm beginning to lose my patience. Dylan, would you tell the class, please?'

'Yes, Mrs Brown. At home, my brothers and I have a special room that is used just for school work. Dad even built each of us a desk of our own and Mum lets us choose what colour we would like it painted. Mine is a sort of light brown with a few spots of cream on it, just like my horse, Rocket.'

'Yeah, yeah. As if! No kid has their own horse, liar.'

'Liam, be quiet. Do that again and you will be spending the rest of the morning in the time-out area.'

'But, Mrs Brown, he ain't got a horse, only them really rich kids have 'em. S'pose he'll tell us that 'is brothers and 'im all got BMX bikes too.'

'Actually we haven't. BMX are a bit too slow around my place and it's too hard to ride in the powdery dirt. But I have got a trail bike. I only hope that my legs get better soon, or maybe I won't ever get to use it again.'

Dylan's face began to crumble and large tears were brimming in his eyes. *Saved*, thought Mrs Brown, as the recess bell broke the uncomfortable silence.

Liam, as always, was first out the door, so he didn't witness Mrs Brown and a few other children trying to comfort Dylan as his tears turned into torrents and his broken little body was racked with sobs.

Later on Dylan's grandmother, Mrs Hunter senior, arrived at the school just as the lunch break had started. She and Mrs Brown almost collided as they both arrived at the office door. Both women wore the same concerned look of maternal instinct for the injured young boy.

'Hello, can I help you?'

'Please, I hope so. I'm Mrs Hunter, Dylan's gran. I've come earlier than I anticipated to take him to the hospital for further assessment, then for physio-treatment.'

'Oh! I'm Mrs Brown, his class-teacher. Dylan was a little upset this morning. Class talk led to horses and bikes and Dylan broke down. Tell me please, there is a good chance he'll regain his strength in his legs again, isn't there? He seems too much of a live wire from his talk this morning to be trapped forever inside his broken body. May I also ask ... ah ... was it your idea to fill in his walking frame?'

'Yes, I thought it would give, umm, what's the saying the youngsters use? A statement to the world, that's it. He intends to recover completely from that dreadful accident and if strong will and determination is needed, he's got more than his share.'

'It's a wonderful idea to put chicken wire around it, easy for attaching things to and those enormous pockets on the inside. I know there are quite a few envious looks from other male members of my class. He seems to have everything at his fingertips in a flash. His pocket treasures have no worry of ending up in the washing machine, like the usual boys jeans pockets.'

'Oh, I am glad you've told me this, because when Dylan first heard what I had in mind, he was afraid the other kids would laugh and make fun of it, even torment him more than ever. I think that's what gets him down the most: not being his own boss anymore, and having to rely on others for basic needs. He was horrified at first, when he realised that someone would have to help wash him for quite some time, instead of jumping in and out of the shower alone.'

Being first out of the classroom at lunchtime had become almost a ritual for Liam, but he had reasons of his own for this. Liam felt he would be letting his tough image slide and perhaps even lose his prestigious place of 'kingpin' amongst his peers. So, as it happened on that fateful day, it was Liam who saw Dylan gradually move off, away from the other class members. All the pupils were required to eat their lunch before a short bell sound signalling that they could begin to move off to start games or just play amongst themselves. Now came the dilemma of which Liam had to make a decision that would ultimately change his life forever.

'Aw geez kid, ya not still sooking about what I said about ya dumb horse are ya?'

An answer never came, and for once Liam held his tongue. Then he saw Dylan's lunch box laying open on the ground. Liam was confused as to why it had been left.

'Look kid … Dilly. Ya sandwiches are drying out sittin' there in the sun. Will I get 'em for ya? Boy, were ya really going to waste this. Hey, ya never ate recess, how ya goen to eat all this?'

'I don't know, I just don't know. Sometimes it's really hard to eat. Gran makes my favourite meals and even cakes, but when I take a mouth full, I just can't swallow it.'

'Dilly, ya lying again, people don't make cakes, ya buy 'em, but only on birthdays or Christmas.'

'But Liam, my Gran really—'

'Dilly, I do … favours sometimes and I usually charge for 'em, but for ya just today, cause ya're new here an all, I'll eat ya lunch, so ya Gran will think ya did. Okay?'

The silence that draped itself around the odd pair of boys was soon consumed by small giggles, coughs and then plain, old-fashioned belly laughs.

'Liam, you don't have to eat so fast. I said I don't want it.'

'Yeah, but mmmmmmm.'

'Liam, what did your mum pack for your lunch?'

'Mmmmmmm, this cake is beautiful, beau ... ti .... ful.'

'It's not cake, silly. That's chocolate slice.'

'Yeah well, I knew that. I had it yesterday. Dilly, can I have that banana for later? 'Cause right now I'm stuffed.'

'Sure Liam, and it was really nice of you, I mean, for you to come and sit with me instead of your friends.'

'Aw, s'nothing, like ya being new and all and not being able to do things for yaself and all. Aw, don't cry, I'm sorry about ya horse, s'pose ya really miss 'im.'

With these few words Liam had touched a fresh raw nerve that Dylan still could not gain control of his emotions.

'Liam do you have any pets?'

'Geez Dilly, ya really are thick. What sort of pets do ya think would like to live where I do? At the moment, I mean. Anyway, I've got things to do, so I'm going now.'

Dylan saw the smallest flash of hurt in his new friend's eyes. *Maybe it was the mention of pets,* he thought.

'Liam. Liam I didn't mean anything. I don't even know where you live. Don't you have much room in your backyard, or is your dad fussy about his garden? My grandy is.'

'Dilly, I sure got ta give ya some learning. Don't ya know anyfing?'

'What do you mean?'

'My dad wouldn't know a garden if it jumped up and bit 'im, and he's never around long enough if he did have one, with all his business things. Backyard, that's a laugh. How can you have somefing of your own, when where ya live is on the tenth floor in a block of units. I mean, that's just for the time being.'

Liam pulled himself up short, thinking, *How does this dumb kid do it? I've never had to explain things to other kids? Maybe it's 'cause he knows I can't whack him.*

'Wow, that's high up. Bet you get a great view. Does your bedroom have a big window, so you can see out while you lay in bed?'

'Oh, oh! This looks like some sort o' trouble brewing.'

Mrs Brown and Mrs Hunter were walking across the playground in the direction of the two boys. They were still deep in conversation with each other.

'I've never seen that 'ol duck before, even if she says it were me. I didn't do it. I ain't never seen 'er.'

'Hey, watch what you say. That's my nana and I think she's the greatest.'

'But she's a grown up. Ya can't never trust 'em, grown-ups, never.'

Dylan could not understand why you couldn't trust adults and was about to ask Liam what he meant, but as he turned around Liam was off at a gallop, leaving Dylan to face the music alone. He never was one for hanging around if he thought trouble was about. The old lady did look sort of nice, not like the ones he talks to outside the Bingo Centre. But then Liam had had some hard lessons learning not to trust adults.

Everyone knew that flowers never grew near the playground, in fact, nowhere at school, but as he ran past there was a definite smell of flowers or something like that. It seemed like a safe distance away now, so Liam turned to see what was happening. That old duck, was she really kissing that dumb kid in the cage? Liam couldn't believe his eyes. Dylan actually put his arms around the old duck and hugged her, right in front of everyone. He sure needed learning about adults.

The trio then headed back towards the classroom and disappeared out of Liam's sight. Out of sight, out of mind. Liam was now getting deeply involved in a game of cricket that needed someone strong, just like him, to see that the rules were enforced especially on those grade six kids, who thought they owned the playground.

For the second time that day the bell signal was a saviour, as a heated difference of opinion was fast turning into a true blue fight about whether it was a six or out.

Days turned into weeks and Dylan was fitting in very nicely, attending class in the morning and treatment in the afternoon. Mrs Hunter Senior was pleased that the lunch box was coming home with only paper, crusts and peel inside. Although she was still very worried and concerned because Dylan was still losing weight. In her mind, he really didn't eat enough at home of proper food, veggies and meat.

Chapter 2

Di Brown had been considering her future about whether to continue working or take the redundancy package being offered. She could not remember the number of times her GP had mentioned lately that she was no longer a 'spring chicken' and she must let others take more of her burden. Had this sudden terrible weighted feeling crept up on her? Or was it because of one pupil by the name of Liam? Oh, what had he done this time? Because of him, stress was now Mrs Brown's constant companion.

'Really, he did. No, I'm not joking. It really was … Liam. I wouldn't have believed it either, if I hadn't seen it myself. He nearly caused a riot, but his intention was good.'

'Okay, what's he done? Do I need to enter it in the discipline book this time?'

'No, no, he insisted that new child in your class – Dylan isn't it? – was the right person to score and make decisions. You know their rules, whether it's a six or out in all those lunch time cricket games.'

There it was again, that flash of a feeling. What was it, what did it mean? Could he really at last be making friends with someone? Dylan would certainly be a steadying influence on Liam. *But then, what would happen when it came time for Dylan to go back to his own family home again?* thought Mrs Brown. The phone in the staffroom began shrieking. Would that new office girl never learn? Lunch time was almost classed as a very sacred time. Where else could one sit in peace and reflect on the horrors of the morning that always seemed to be unending? So, why couldn't that girl just take messages as she did during class time?

'Mrs Brown. Mrs Di Brown wanted on line three,' bellowed the public address system.

'Hello, Mrs Brown speaking. Yes. No, I don't mind you calling, Mrs Hunter. Liam, yes he's a boy in my class. Oh dear, what's he done?'

'No, no Mrs Brown, I'm ringing to thank you. It must have been something you've said. Dylan's finally coming out into the real world again. I had begun to think he'd never find fun in anything ever again. Now, all I hear about is Liam did this, Liam said that.'

'Yes. Oh, thanks, Mrs Hunter, thanks. But I'm really not the cause of his improvement. Mrs Hunter, you mentioned Liam. I hope he hasn't been tormenting or causing trouble for Dylan?'

'No. Far from it. Dylan wants to visit Liam this coming Saturday. So I presumed, or rather hoped, that you could fill me in on the family. I already know from Dylan that Mr Sims has a job that takes him away a lot, and that they're living in a unit while their home is being renovated and the pool is being extended to include a spa pool.'

"Whaaat? What did you say Mrs Hunter?'

'I hope I didn't shock you. You sound surprised. When my children were young, it was quite acceptable to enquire from the teacher if your child wished to visit a family that you had never made acquaintances with before. Is that not allowed today? I'm very sorry, I just didn't think, but then, everybody seems so preoccupied with privacy today.'

'Oh dear. Oh dear, Mrs Hunter. I hate being the bearer of bad news, but more so I may be the one person that will deflate the new-found confidence your grandson finds so much pleasure and friendship in.'

'Mrs Brown can't you bend the rules, just this once? No, not for me, but for the boy, please do it for Dylan.'

'No. No, it's not that. In fact, I really think, if you are willing to meet me for coffee this evening, there are one or two things about this situation that I now feel you should be aware of. No, nothing we can't handle, but you need to know things and I can't explain it over the phone. Seven-thirty at Maxine's in the High Street Arcade, great. See you then. Bye, Mrs Hunter.'

How Di Brown taught her class during the afternoon she had no idea, because her mind kept wandering back to what Mrs Hunter had said. It was certainly going to take a lot of tact and diplomacy to somehow explain the Sims family situation.

Chapter 3

'Hell, Dilly, do ya really 'ave to be *that* honest?'

'What do you mean, Liam?'

'Do I 'ave ta spell it out? Gee, Dilly, ya really ain't had much education have ya? Air school might be okay for some things, but no way with cricket rules. We would've had 'em creamed if ya'd given 'im out instead of a flamin' six. I don't want ta play any more anyway.'

'Liam. No, wait up Liam. Ooooooh, aaaah.'

Dylan was in such a hurry to patch things up with his friend, for a moment he had actually forgotten about his damn legs. The built up momentum was too much to control and over he went. Small boy, walking frame, better known as 'the cage', treasures and the score book were now all in such a tangled mess on the ground. The sudden excitement caused a crowd to gather and the sounds of dozens of children's voices soon grew in volume. Miss Dickson had noticed Dylan and Liam having, what seemed to her, some sort of disagreement. So, rightly or wrongly, she had already more or less mentally accused Liam of being the cause of what ever had happened.

'Liam, go to the office now, and wait there 'til I help Dylan to the sick-bay.'

'But. Miss Dickson, but I was only—'

'Liam. Go, now.'

'Geez, a kid can't do anyfing right. Damn teachers.'

'Dylan are you hurt? Can you move? No. No, I mean shouldn't you be staying still. Oh dear, you're not bleeding are you?'

'No, Miss Dickson, and Liam was really—'

'Don't worry, Dylan. I'll sort Liam out. This will probably mean a hefty suspension this time.'

'No, no. Oh, Miss Dickson, no.'

'Ssshh … Dylan, don't get so worked up. It'll be alright, really it will.'

'But, you don't understand, Miss Dickson. He—'

'Liam's been heading for this for weeks now.'

'But …'

She would not listen to the boy as she and some helpers gathered Dylan and all his bits and pieces together before heading off towards the sickbay area.

'Please, Miss Dickson, it was not Liam's fault, he was only helping—'

'It's alright, Dylan, the headmaster will sort it out this time. Liam is his own worst enemy.'

'Um … Nurse, take care of this pupil please until his grandmother comes to collect him.'

'Yes, Angie–I mean Miss Dickson.'

It was really hard to address a friend in a formal manner, but as she was only new at the school she supposed it would get easier.

'Hi, there. You're Dylan, aren't you? So now, do you want to tell me how all this happened and where it hurts?'

'Yes, Miss. Nothing happened really, but Miss Dickson wouldn't listen. We were just having our cricket game and

I scored a six for the other team when Liam was sure it was out. Then I forgot about my back and legs and turned quickly to go after Liam to explain and I fell in a heap. Please go and say something to Miss Dickson before Liam is in any more trouble, 'cause this time it was not his fault.'

'I see. You care a lot for your new friend, don't you, Dylan?'

'Yes I do. Now, can you help both of us?'

chapter 4

Maxine's was a good venue to meet and discuss what was causing a great deal of anxiety for Mrs Brown. Mrs Hunter Senior seemed almost foreign to the usual parent that Mrs Brown was used to dealing with on school or personal matters. How could she ever express her true feelings and knowledge of the Sims family? Mrs Hunter was a true lady and it would or could cause her too much anguish to hear the truth about Liam. No, somehow Mrs Brown knew that she had to explain the situation but she would just have to choose her words carefully and watch for clues from Mrs Hunter incase it became more difficult than Mrs Brown believed it would be for Mrs Hunter to accept.

The patrons using Maxine's tonight were certainly a lively bunch, very pleasant, high spirited but suitably well behaved. *Dear, dear,* she thought, *I really must get out more often, imagine thinking of these people in the same context as I would a class at school.* Now, what was Liam's favourite saying? That's it, 'Get a life.'

Her eyes travelled the room and rested on the clock behind the counter. It was already seven-forty-five. Had she put too much intrigue in the phone call she'd exchanged with Mrs Hunter? The waitress appeared for the second time, only to be dismissed again without an order. Di's mind began its wandering, as it did quite regularly, through the worlds of 'what if' and 'if onlys,' so much so that she was startled back to the here and now by a voice nearby.

'Good evening, Mrs Brown. Sorry, I'm a bit late. Dylan was most concerned that tonight was going to cause more trouble for Liam. It's really not, is it? It was the last thing he wanted for Liam, to get into any more trouble.'

'Heavens, no. Quite the reverse I feel.'

'Oh good, Dylan insisted that he'd read in bed until I got home. I just hope he and his grandfather can hold their concern 'til then.'

'Sounds to me like young Liam has caused your family to worry, but then I guess Liam seems to have a natural ability to do that to people he meets.'

'May I take your order now?' the waitress asked in a somewhat brusque manner.

'Sorry, yes, I'll have cappuccino and cheesecake. How about you Mrs Hunter? It's my shout. The cheesecakes are really delightful and I think we can do with something sweet to help us through the conversation we are going to be having.'

'Well, yes. Thank you and please call me Marie. Mrs Hunter sounds too formal for a meeting such as ours.'

'Great, and please call me Di, or Dianne if you prefer. It's really nice to have a break away from the mundane side of teaching, marking books can sometimes be such a chore.'

'Do you really find teaching a bit hard to handle sometimes? I suppose it does take up a lot of your social time, especially with interfering parents and grandparents like myself.'

'No, no, it's nice to have someone take a bit more notice about what's going on.'

Both women sat enjoying the atmosphere, coffee and cake and, more importantly, each other's company until Marie could contain her curiosity no longer.

'Dianne – I mean Di – what was it you could not tell me on the phone about Liam? There's no serious illness I should be aware of is there? I wouldn't like Dylan to be pushing into a family crisis.'

'No. Well, no. Oh, Marie, how do I start to tell you?'

'I knew it. I just knew it. When I asked Dylan what his friend Liam was like he was always evasive or just changed the subject. I just can't get more than the yes or no answer.'

'Dear, oh dear. I feel it's partly my fault. I should have seen these problems coming, but well, no one has ever been able to become a *real* friend to Liam. I was just so pleased for Liam, that I'd never thought past Dylan being a school-hours friend. You see, Liam never lets people get too close to him. I think it's ... ah, like a self protection insurance he carries. We at school only ever see the very tip of the iceberg where Liam is concerned. Oh Marie, by the expression on your face, I'm not really making things any better am I?'

'Di, from what I've gathered this problem is a serious one, isn't it? Even more than I first thought with your strange phone conversation. How about I get us both another coffee? And you won't, I promise you, shock me about families. Please, start at the beginning and let's see if a solution can be worked out. Two heads are supposed to be better than one.'

Chapter 5

'Grandy, it's really okay if you want to go back to the loungeroom to watch your programs. Current affair shows always seem to be about the same things to me – doom and gloom – and I'd rather read a couple more chapters of my library book.'

'Dylan, how about we turn off the television and you put down your book and we'll have a man-to-man talk while Nana is spending time with your teacher ... What's her name?'

'Mrs Brown, Grandy.'

'Oh yeah, that's it.'

Mr John Hunter had imagined all sorts of things that would not be good for his grandson. These days you just couldn't be sure of anyone's intentions. Even people you thought you knew. John had certainly run into some strange characters whilst tracking down missing links in his passion, family histories.

'Dylan, what do you know of this new friend of yours, Liam, isn't it? I mean you have never spoken about his family or what they do, you know, man stuff?'

'Gee Grandy. I didn't think you were nosy. You always say that's Nana's job, don't you?'

'Hey boy, I know I suggested us having a man talk, but that doesn't mean respect goes out the door. Your Nana's really worried about your new friend. That's why she's gone out tonight meeting with Mrs Brown.'

'I'm sorry, really I am, but sometimes I just get sick and tired of everyone worrying about my feelings. It's my legs and back that are injured, not how I think.'

'That's the spirit, boy. Stand up for what you believe in. Sometimes when you're older you forget how you youngsters grow up, faster than the years travel. Must be old age. We're not really being nosy, your Nana and I. It's a big responsibility to see to your welfare while you're away from your mum and dad. I suppose sometimes I forget it's you and think about David, your father, when he was your age. Truth be, I reckon you've got more spunk than he ever had.'

At this, Dylan's saucer-sized eyes were rapidly filling with tears. Not really of hurt, but of pride, because he really loved his father and it hurt a real lot being away from his family.

The sight was too much for John. He never had been able to cope with full on emotion. He'd always left that to Marie.

Dylan picked up his book almost at the same time as John rose to leave his grandson's room. Neither of them knew quite what to do with the feelings they were experiencing. It just wasn't manly, was it?

'Goodnight, Grandy. Ask Nana to come in when she gets home, please. I want to know what happened.'

'Yeah. Well yeah Dylan, I will. Ah, goodnight boy.'

Dylan had his book open, but his mind was transporting his broken body back home, where he felt the freedom of a great open space of the cattle station instead of the closed in feeling he was experiencing whilst living in the city. He felt so hemmed in some days that he was sure if he had to live here all the time he'd lose his mind. Dylan now thought of Rocket. Who would be giving him special treats or rubbing him between his ears? Maybe his brothers were, but Rocket would know the difference. Perhaps he was beginning to forget all about the attention Dylan gave him. With that thought, Dylan covered his eyes with his arm and gently cried until he had no longer the strength to keep awake until Nana came home.

Chapter 6

'Marie, what I'm about to tell you must stay just between us. I don't make a practise of disclosing details contained in pupil files. The headmaster has agreed in this instance because without this knowledge you and, of course, Dylan could end up in a very sticky situation that would turn into embarrassment for all concerned. Liam as well.

'It all began to unravel when you mentioned Mr Sims' work. You see, he's a habitual petty criminal. I don't think he has ever done an honest day's work in his entire life. Don't get me wrong, he is a very pleasant person and a wonderful loving father. From what I can gather, he dropped out of high school after numerous lengths of suspension. That's another reason why I strive so hard to look after Liam's' welfare. Nothing serious to start with, a bit like his son, full of hijinks and game for any dare, but a bit hard to control. Then, things started to go missing, you know, small things: lunches, items of clothing, books and spare change pupils left unattended. Suspicion always fell on him but nothing could ever be proven, even then he was a master at covering his tracks. Then, as history has it, a new family moved into the area, a church sponsored refugee family from a storm ravaged tropical island somewhere in the South Pacific. From all accounts, the only daughter was exquisite, a real beauty to behold and had brains to match. But she was absolutely spoilt rotten by her father and her three brothers. Well, from that first day, Master Ronald Sims was spell bound; you could say that his soul was a captive to the beauty of this light coffee-coloured girl with long silken hair that had a radiance that turned many heads. If the complication between those two happened a generation later, many lives would not share the unfortunate circumstances that Liam now lives every moment of his life.

'As you have undoubtedly guessed, Master Ronald and Mistress Leila found themselves unconditionally bound together in a tantalising summer love of youthful emotions.

'By the time Leila realised the few extra kilos were not entirely due to lack of physical exercise or the countless thick shakes she and Ronald shared, others too had their suspicions. Both were still dreaming of their wonderful future together, but elsewhere their bubble was exploding already, as the parents had guessed the hideous, to their thinking, outcome of Leila's future. Leila had won an expensive scholarship to an exclusive all-girls' school for the next two years and if she kept her grades up, she knew that she would easily take a place in the law faculty at university. This thought had even sparked a learning flame back into Ronald's mind, because Leila had promised to help him with his subjects, and Ronald thought, hadn't Leila taught him so much already this summer? Life was really a great adventure.

Leila had been taken to the local doctor firstly because of her fathers' horrific suspicions, and secondly of her mothers' concern that Leila could keep nothing down in the mornings, not even water. When the results were given, the parents were heartbroken, especially her father. That young drifter had violated his daughter, his princess. But Leila would have nothing nasty said about Ronald; in fact, she wanted and welcomed his baby.'

Chapter 7

'Hello, Mr Sims. I'm ringing about your son, Ronald. No, no there's been no accident. Well, not really. Your son's fine, for now anyway.'

'What? What do you mean? Mr … Sorry, I didn't catch your name.'

'Mr Phillips. John Phillips. I organise sponsorships for refugee families.'

'Yeah well, that's fine. I don't give to foreign charities. And anyway Ronnie's not in need of any charity neither.'

'Oh. Just a minute, Mr Sims. I haven't made myself very clear.'

'No! You're right on that score, mate.'

'Mr Sims, please listen carefully. What I need to tell you is somewhat delicate. With all the previous refugee families I've never had to discuss this subject.'

'Look mate, spit it out whatever the subject, because I'm losing my patience.'

'Well it's … it's about Leila.'

'About who? Who the hell's Leila?'

'The daughter of my refugee family.'

'Oh. You mean that bit of coloured fluff that seems to have been a permanent attachment to Ronnie's arm? Ronnie sure had fun this summer. It's the first summer holiday that the coppers haven't been round here hounding me about the boy, saying he's the cause of some trouble about the neighbourhood.'

'Yes, Mr Sims but … I'm sorry there is trouble. There's no easy way for me to say this.'

'Geez, Phillips. You're starting to really annoy me.'

'Mr Sims. Leila is *pregnant*!'

'So …'

'Mr Sims, it's because of your son Ronald.'

'Never. Geez. I really hadn't thought of him other than a curious boy. Well, how about that, Ronnie's going to be a father.'

'Yes, Mr Sims, but here's the problem. What is to become of them? You see, Mr Tanekaha, Leila's father, is too shocked. He won't have her in the family home. She was his very existence, his world, and now she's expecting your son's child.'

Now the reality of the situation began to slowly sink into the depths of Mr Sims' mind. It was clear to him that there was no real drama. He'd go and see this fluffs' father and explain the situation. *Ronnie is in no position to become a parent, so I'll pay for the girl to wait out her time in one of those places.* The places where loose girls had to go when they got caught with a child. It would be a shame to never know his first grandchild, but he was sure Ronnie would settle down one day. Marry and raise a family. Yes, that was a good way out, no drama.

Mr Phillips just couldn't see his way out of trouble like he was able to. There would be a bit of expense, he thought, but then the nuns make those girls repent for their mistake by doing manual work for their keep. Mr Sims knew all about this because his mate, Curly, had a niece that got herself caught. *The girls of today just don't know how to behave, they get caught and then lay all the blame on the fella.* Two hundred dollars, that would be a fair price of offer to the fluff's father and if he started to get nasty he'd raise it to two-fifty ... *top dollar.*

Mr Sims took quite a while to gather the two hundred dollars together, so it was some weeks, maybe a couple of months, before he actually went to see the girl's father. He went straight from work, not even thinking of the impression his appearance would have on her parents. He knew he always looked a bit grimy after working the boilers at the foundry all day, but geez, it was good honest work.

His third knock was answered and the horrified look on the woman's face told him he should have come in the evening, after getting cleaned up a bit.

'Hi, I'm Ron. Ron Sims ...'

Now a man appeared behind the woman. 'Leave,' he shouted. 'Leave and never return. You and your son have ruined my family.'

'Now, just a mo', mate.'

'Leave, before I get the police.'

'Okay, okay, keep your hair on. I was just going to offer you a couple of hundred for her trouble, and I know a place where she can go before it's born and then they'll take care of it for her. No worries.'

Now the man screamed even louder, 'Get out of my sight.' He slammed the door shut in Ron's face.

'Well, you just can't help some people,' Ron said to himself out loud as he walked back to his car parked further down the street.

Chapter 8

'So you see, Marie, out of all this confusion, Liam was the result. Not a very nice way to start your existence in the world. Yes, Ronald and Leila did get married, but the details I've got are only hearsay and not especially nice. You can understand, family feuds and that sort of thing. Liam pictures his family by way of make-believe; maybe it's his way of coping with a very dysfunctional family. Because Liam is the eldest, he's been given too much responsibility in regard to his siblings.'

In Di Brown's mind, anyone who was expected to have children as nature predicted, just to satisfy church rules, was either stupid or brainwashed. Everyone knew Leila was not stupid. Someday, missionaries who interfere with another's race beliefs, superstitions or rituals will be asked to explain their reasoning. It seemed that the entire time Mrs Brown had known the Sims family, they were celebrating a birth or the forthcoming expectancy.

Liam, nine and a half years; Suzy, eight years; twin boys, seven years; girl, five years; boy, four years; twin girls, two and a half years; unborn twins.

It was no wonder Mrs Sims had increased to the obese size she now was. Her poor body never seemed to get a rest from producing and nurturing her youngsters. Ronald Sims did try hard in the beginning of the enforced marriage, but Leila had never wanted for anything in her entire life and even though she was very bright, housework and cooking meals seemed to cause only confusion to her. So much so that each day of their married life she seemed to do less and less.

Ronald's jobs were always of low-paid variety because he'd messed about at school and failed to pass the required exams. Not long after the birth of the twin boys, Ronald was befriended by a handsome dark-haired young man who'd moved into the unit next door. Fate played a hand in their friendship.

Leila used to have the voice of an angel, but since that very bad bout of flu, she sounded more like a strangled rooster. So, it was fate that the voice and the mess had caused Ronald to be on the stairs outside the unit when Angelo was having a hard time moving his gear into his unit. The total amazement on Ronald's face was quickly noted by the newcomer and over a glass of rough red to wash down a pizza, a dubious friendship was cemented in mateship.

Angelo's uncle owned the pizza shop in the shopping mall and he was away travelling a lot on business. Angelo was more or less the boss. The offer of a bit of spare work and free pizza was snapped up very quickly by Ronald. His conscience was swept away with this slippery, street-wise young man.

In his heart. Ronnie knew that no good would come from this friendship, but sometimes one just doesn't have a choice, one just has to provide for his family the best way he could. Occasionally, Ronnie was tempted to open the sealed pizza box just to see for himself what he was really delivering. Nothing but pizza and the foil wrapped garlic bread. Why then, he wondered, was it his job to take them personally to what Ronnie thought exclusive addresses? Not your regular pizza-eating people, and the money was always given to him in a sealed envelope. Something else that puzzled him: there was usually a couple of middle-aged men present with four or five young girls. But what the heck, the pay was good and the tips from these addresses were extraordinarily high.

For a time Leila was pleased with what she now had: a husband with two jobs, pizza, garlic bread and Coke laid on. All this changed in an instant when she realised that once again she was pregnant. This just could not happen. At times like this, she wished she could talk with her mum. Neither Leila nor Ronnie could envisage what lay in store for them. When the doctor told Leila that she was expecting twins again, she took to her bed and stayed there, only occasionally seeing to the children. Ronnie was told in no uncertain terms that he'd have to look after the children because Leila was too tired. Ronnie's daytime job fizzled out because of his absenteeism, so he spent more nights at the pizza shop with Angelo. Now came the beginning of his life of petty crime, as he helplessly watched his beautiful wife turn into a human blimp.

Marie and Di were both startled by the waitress enquiring about whether they wished for more coffee, and that she was sorry, but it was almost time to close-up for the night.

'Oh my goodness, Di, it's eleven-thirty. Where did the evening go? I do hope Dylan has gone to sleep, I don't think I could handle a third degree conversation with him tonight. It will be hard enough with the questions that undoubtedly will be formed by my husband.'

'Yes, Marie, I understand how you feel. But then I suppose I'm lucky because my house companion always listens intently to what I say, never interrupts, and asks only that I provide meals and to share my bed. But then I'm so used to his company I don't think I could sleep now, without his hypnotic purring as I gently stroke his fur.'

<h1 style="text-align:center">chapter 9</h1>

'Gee, Dilly, I don't know what ya told Miss Dickson, but I didn't even get a detention for whatever that old lady said I'd done.'

'Liam, I told you before, she's my Nana and she is really great. Maybe I'll ask if you can—'

'See ya, Dilly. I've got to have a few words with that new kid over there. Back in a mo'.'

Dylan had noticed that any time he had tried to get an answer from Liam, he seemed to close up and do something else or, as had happened now, just rush off somewhere else. His brother William was very good at doing the same thing. Dylan could never understand why, but then his brother William was the eldest and he didn't see any need for Dylan to know all the in's and out's of the cattle station. Perhaps if he'd talked a bit more of the dangers, the accident might never have happened.

Sitting at their desks, Dylan asked again, 'Liam I'm going to ask Nana if you could come round on a Saturday.'

'I'd like that Dilly, but … I dunno, me dad doesn't like it if I'm not round to help Mam with the rest of the kids on weekends.'

'Liam, do you ever wish you could go somewhere or do something that you know you can't?'

'Ya sure say strange things, Dilly.'

'But … don't you? I mean, I make wishes every day now.'

'Do ya, Dilly? And here I thought you had it all. Like ya got a horse and a trail bike. Now, I know for sure I'll never have things like that, no matter how 'ard I wish.'

'Liam, what if my back and legs *never* get right? I'll never be able to face living like this forever.'

'*Don't*. Don't say fings like that. I've never had someone like ya for a friend before. I'd hate it if ya weren't around.'

Dylan made a quick rush for the tissues in the side pocket of his cage, just as Liam was about to make a quick exit because he just couldn't stand to see his friend in so much anguish.

Liam was now running so hard and his own tears were blinding him so, that he didn't have time to see the four grade six boys moving the hockey goal net ready for the game that afternoon. The noise and commotion startled everyone. Two of the older boys were busy trying to control their nose bleeds and it took a moment to realise that there was a small body trapped under the tangle of rope, pipes and netting. Miss Dickson and Mrs Brown arrived simultaneously from opposite directions.

'What on earth? How did this happen?'

'It wasn't our fault. Liam just ran into us. He hasn't moved since.'

'Okay, okay. Harry, you and Eric had better both go and see the school nurse, just in case. Although you both look as though you've been very lucky, to have suffered no great harm. Kevin and James sit down there against the wall, at least until your noses ease up a bit. Oh, James, looks as though you'll have a real shiner tomorrow. Liam, can you hear me? No, don't try to move, just wait till the stretcher gets here.'

'Stretcher! I don't need no stretcher. I'm not a sissy. Ooooooooooh, aaaaaaaah. Oh, me arm 'urts and so does me leg.'

'Yes, Liam, I reckon it does.'

'Mrs Brown, Mrs Brown what happened to Liam? Is he hurt really bad?'

'Not sure yet, Dylan. Do you know why he was running so fast without looking?'

'Ah … maybe. I'm not sure.'

'It's okay, Dilly. I'm not too bad. But it sure 'urts like hell when I try to move. Mrs Brown, can Dilly stay 'ere with me? I know the bell's gone and all, but can he please?'

Amid all the drama, nobody noticed that Mrs Hunter had arrived to collect Dylan for his usual treatment time at the hospital.

'No, Nana, you go in the car. I'm going with Liam in the ambulance. You see, he's really scared and he just doesn't trust adults. I'll come round to the physio department as soon as Liam's alright.'

'Dylan, I don't know if that's a good thing. Really, a teacher should be with him.'

'Hello, Mrs Hunter.'

'Hello, Mrs Brown. How's Liam? Dylan seems to think he's travelling in the ambulance with him.'

'Well, no. I mean, I'm going, but Liam got so anxious one of the ambulance men thought it was a good idea to keep him calm, if his best mate went with him, too. Poor Liam, he's terrified.'

Once Liam was settled in the back of the ambulance he seemed to regain some of his cocky spirit.

'Hey mate, could ya please put the lights and siren on, just as we drive along the main street. I ain't never been in an ambulance before and probably won't never again neither.'

'Look, it's really not allowed.'

'Please, mate,' pleaded Liam.

'Okay. But not until we're past the shops. How about from the hotel to the police station?'

'Yeah. Me dad might even hear me goin' past.'

'But Liam, he'll come to the hospital as soon as the school lets him know.'

"Nah, not 'im Dilly. Me dad hates hospitals. He don't even go to see me Mam when she has the babies.'

'It's okay Liam, Nana's waiting at the hospital. It's my treatment time and after it's finished I'll come back to casualty and sit with you. Mrs Brown will be there too.'

Chapter 10

Mrs Brown was gently telling herself, *take a deep breath, count to ten and turn the anxiety off.* She knew Liam was going to need her strength tonight. Sitting waiting in the confined space of the cubical neither pupil or teacher had any idea what lay ahead.

'Mrs Brown, where'd they put me jeans?'

'It's all right Liam, you won't be wearing them tonight.'

'Yeah, but ...'

'Liam, try and stay still.'

'But, but I want to see what's goin' on. Who's mak'n' all that damn noise?'

How could someone with suspected fractures be wriggling around that much? While she continued sitting, watching and waiting, her gaze was brought to a mind stopping halt – as the gown Liam now wore slipped, thus exposing the tanned, somewhat muscled back of a youth on the verge of starting his growth into manhood.

'Liam. How – I mean who – What has happened to your back?'

Being unused to close scrutiny of adult eyes, Liam was shocked into a silent stillness that was not only foreign to him, but his teacher who was now his companion for the night as well. He was trying desperately to join the hospital gown together and erase the last few minutes.

'Liam, dear. Oh, I'm sorry. I wasn't prying. It's just … Well, injuries like that …'

'*No,*' he shouted with such force and anger. 'No, Mrs Brown. It's nuffin' really. In fact, none of your business. I'm sorry, Mrs Brown, really I am, but I ain't got nuffin' to say to no one.'

'Oh Liam, I only want to help you. When the doctor sees it he'll want some answers and he'll insist.'

'When's Dilly getting here? I'm gitt'en bored. I want to go home.'

'Yes dear, it must seem like ages, waiting. I think that's one of the biggest problem people find in hospitals, waiting. Waiting to get in, waiting to be seen, waiting for a bed, waiting to be able to go to the bathroom.'

'Aww, Mrs Brown … Did ya hav'ta? Where is it? I've really got to go *bad.*'

As he said it, the doctor finally ducked through the cubicle curtain.

'Sims, Liam Sims. Which cubical did you say, Nurse? You must be Sims. Ah, and you are his mother, yes?'

'Geez, git real Doc, that's not me mam, that's me teacher.'

'Oh, sorry, mate, bad mistake.'

'No, not really. Mrs Brown's cool, for a teacher I mean.'

'Well, let's take a look at you, old man.'

'But only me arm and me leg. *Nothing* else, see.'

Four adult eyes connected instantly, two with a look of worry, the other two with surprise. What was going to be the ultimate outcome of the next few minutes? Perhaps long awaited help for a young boy, who, through his self-pride, could not obtain alone. Perhaps it was a blessing in disguise as the hidden problem was being taken out of Liam's hands. Maybe Liam's feeling of helplessness involving the boy named Hill, would now be coming to an end.

'Sims, old man. I don't know what you think I'm going

to do to you. My main job here is to help and take care of people.'

'Look, Doc. I just don't want you or nobody else gawking at me body. It's only me leg and me arm that got hurt.'

'Okay, all right old man. Ummm, Mrs Brown could you please give us men a few minutes alone, some people's beautiful bodies just aren't meant for the eyes of the public.'

'But of course, I should have realised Liam wouldn't want his teacher knowing that he has warts on his chest and long black hair on his back.'

'Yeah, yeah, Mrs Brown, as if …'

Di Brown was actually relieved to be free of the small cubical, even though she knew she would soon be called upon for any answers she could give. Her mind was racing with thoughts of how and why Liam bore those scars in secret. It couldn't have been his mum; she was big and strong, yes, but she really loves her son. Mr Sims, well, he was a lazy good-for-nothing, but she could not imagine him as a bully, more of a stray pussycat really. Di really couldn't imagine that if Liam had been in serious trouble or being harassed and bullied, that he would have stayed so silent for so long.

Chapter 11

John had not even noticed it was well past the time Marie said she'd be home after having coffee with Dylan's teacher. However, time meant nothing when he surrounded himself with his charts and notes. The soft click of the key in the lock and the unforgiving creak as the door opened suddenly brought his thoughts back from his beloved branches of his family tree. John Hunter enjoyed his time fiddling with his snippets of history. His grandchildren would say, 'Oh, Grandy's playing with his old names again', but at least his knowledge had proved very helpful to numerous people who sought out his advice when they were attempting their own family history. There was many a family he had researched for relatives and friends that built up a wonderful foundation of local roots and also those of far away.

'Oh, hi Marie. What's wrong? You look exhausted.'

'Really, John, do you always have to state the very obvious?'

'Sorry, dear. I'll go and put the kettle on, you'll enjoy your cuppa.'

'Thanks John. Is Dylan asleep, I hope?'

'Yes. I looked in a while ago, he's dead to the world.'

Soon the cups were filled with chamomile tea and the pieces of raisin bread that John had toasted were oozing butter. But no one was watching calories tonight.

'Marie, how about we take this lot to the bedroom and you can then totally relax in bed whilst enjoying your cuppa.'

'John, you are a treasure. Really you are.'

It wasn't until John and Marie were cuddled up together that Marie started retelling the horrors and dreams that are the foundation of the little being named Liam.

'John, do you think … Could there be …'

'Yes, Marie. I've been waiting for this subject to come up since Dylan first started talking about his new-found friend. What sort of plan is smouldering away in that head of yours this time?'

'Really, John. I do wish you wouldn't make me sound so predictable, you couldn't possibly know what I was going to suggest.'

'Alright, for starters, Liam coming here for a visit, perhaps the boys could spend some time together during the holidays. Maybe we'd get to know Liam's family.'

'Okay, okay, point taken. John, could we? I mean, what you said was really the plan I was hatching. I just don't understand how you know what I'm thinking.'

'Maybe it's all the practise I've had during the past forty-five years. In fact, I bet right now you're thinking of the wonderful way I always kiss away your troubles at the end of each day.'

John moved over and gently put his arm around Marie, at the same time turning out the light.

'Goodnight. Yes, I do love the way we're always at peace come the end of the day.'

There were no nightmares stalking about in the depths of their dream state. Unlike some other disturbed members of the sleeping town, where darkness brought out their worst fears and horrors.

Chapter 12

'Mrs Sims, hello. It's Miss Dickson from the school.'

'For gawdsake. be quiet. Sorry. Sometimes I can't hear myself think with the kids. Now, what's the problem there, dearie? Anyone would think you teachers really have it in for my Liam.'

'No. Mrs Sims, it's nothing like that.'

'Well, what is it then? Hey, don't hit your sister like that!'

'Mrs Sims, is there anyone that could mind your children for a while?'

'What the hell for? You teachers sometimes go too far.'

At this point in the conversation, Angie Dickson realised why no one else had been very eager to notify Mrs Sims about the accident.

'No, no Mrs Sims. There's been an accident. Liam's at the hospital.'

'Suzy get down from there. What did you say? What sort of accident? Is my Liam hurt real bad? Look dear, I could never go to the hospital with this tribe, and Ronnie won't be home for hours, if then even.'

'I'm sorry, Mrs Sims, but I don't know the state of his injuries. It did look as though his leg may be broken, and maybe his shoulder, too. I'm not sure.'

'Tell me dear, was it anything to do with that new kid?'

'Dylan? No, Dylan wasn't the cause.'

'Oh not 'im. The other bigger boy. Someone Hills, I think Liam called 'im. Liam gets quite upset, even uncontrollably angry, whenever he comes round here.'

'No, I'm sorry, I don't know of that boy.'

'No matter, dear, Ronnie's said he'll sort 'im out.'

'Mrs Sims, would it help if I came round and stayed with your children, while you go to Liam? Mrs Brown is with him at the moment, but I'm sure he'd be relieved to have his mum there too.'

'Gee that's really kind of you, dear. Most people shy away from me and me kids, they think we're strange and a bit wild. You see, not many families have eight littlies and another on the way, er ... I mean two on the way.'

'I'll be round in say, forty minutes to an hour. I'm finished with my classroom duties, but I've just got to finish writing up the incident report form. It's formality to do it correctly and straight away. Bye, Mrs Sims.'

'Yes, bye. And thanks ever so much, dear.'

Miss Dickson heard the dial tone ringing away in her ear, as her mind was running a one minute mile. Had she done the right thing in offering assistance or had her kind and giving nature been let down by her quick talking mouth? No, her belief was that whatever you give out will one day return when you are in need. Miss Dickson thought back to her own childhood for a moment. Life in the orphanage had been a rude awakening to her quiet life before the tragic death of her parents, but she had coped and now she had personal experience in crowd control of excited unruly children.

Miss Dickson had been lucky to find a park for her car in a busy, well-lit area close to the block of units where she busily unloaded her belongings. She wondered whether Mrs Sims would take offence at her bringing a sleeping bag, change of clothing and a few necessary items of food. Life in her crowded childhood and again in teachers college had taught her to take a few liberties and always be prepared when dealing with an unknown situation. This situation was a classic for her social welfare studies course she was doing on a part-time basis at the local university.

'Aw Mam, 'snot fair, we want ta go with ya.'

'Well, ya not.'

'But Da's not home. Who's gunna watch us?'

'No one.'

'Aw, Mam.'

'Shut up you lot, there's someone at the door.'

Miss Dickson was all prepared to meet the Sims tribe, but even her spartan upbringing couldn't prepare her for what she saw as the door opened. The stale air assault on her nose was almost unbearable, lingering food and body odour all mixed up together. Did they all use the lounge room floor as a communal clothes storage area? How did they ever choose a pair of shoes from the dozens piled up in the corner? Everywhere she let her eyes travel there seemed dirt and grime, washed and unwashed clothing, garbage bags lined up like soldiers, and little bodies. There seemed to be children peeping out from behind furniture everywhere she looked.

'Hello, Miss Dickson. Look, it's really nice of you to offer to stay, but are you sure you'll be able to cope? I mean, I know my kids and what they can get up to.'

'Think nothing of it, Mrs Sims. Hey, are you feeling okay? You don't look the best.'

'No, I'm fine. But I think maybe the shock about Liam may have hastened the arrival time of our next additions.'

'You mean … um, you think it's time? What do I do?'

'Don't worry yourself, I'm well practised by now.'

'Yes, but Mr Sims, where can I get in touch with him for you?'

'Don't worry, my Ronnie doesn't like this part. He'll see me, when I return home again.'

'At least let me organise a ride for you or call an ambulance.'

'All done. After your phone call, I rang the Women's Centre and they should have a volunteer on the way to pick me up. They also said they'd be only too glad to give you a hand with the tribe. Number's stuck on the fridge. Oh, here they are now.

'Oh, Miss Dickson. Just one word of warning: don't let 'em outside. They'll go in all directions and you'll never round 'em up again. Thanks ever so much for your help.'

Angie Dickson, what have you got yourself into now? Tears are going to be useless so come on girl, pull yourself together, and do what you can to help these youngsters. She also thought it had really been great insight to carry all the gear up in stages and leave it in the hall outside, because there was no way she could have left the children to get it.

Chapter 13

'Okay troops, now it's time to start our very own game.'
'Hey missus, we're not 'oops.'

'Oh, sorry. Here, I'll start again. Until Liam and your mum come home this place is going to be our own island and we have to look after it and each other. We'll pretend we're an army guarding the land from outsiders. The only people that can come in are your dad, the king, and a couple of my friends who are going to help me look after you. Everyone else is the enemy.'

'I'm gunna make water bombs.'

'No, sorry. We're not that kind of army, we don't have guns or bombs.'

'Really? How we gunna keep the enemy out then?'

'Some of the enemy we can't see, like …'

'That's silly. I don't wanta play.'

'Okay, but that means you have to be the army's prisoner and prisoners are not allowed to do anything. No drinking, eating, sleeping, talking, reading and especially no telly.'

'Sounds like I'd have ta be dead.'

'Do you want to join in then?'

'Yeah I s'pose, but how do we find the enemy?'

'First, everyone who's no older than Liam, must have a bath and wash their hair and clean their teeth.'

'How come?'

'Because that's how we're going to catch the enemy. Girls can share the bath first, followed by the boys. I'll help by bathing the toddlers.'

'What's in all them boxes and bags.'

'Army rations.'

'Army who?'

'Things that the army issues to the soldiers. Here girls, pink bubble bath for you, and somewhere there's blue for the boys. Because we're going to be a team, I've brought a track suit for everyone. I hope I guessed the right sizes. This is so we can all look the same, like soldiers do.'

'Yeah … But your skin is different and you've got light coloured hair, not black like ours and our skin's brown, not like yours.'

'But I'm the one who has to be responsible, you know. I take the blame if anything goes wrong. If I had black hair too, we might all get confused as to who to blame.'

'Oh … you mean like Da. He has different hair and skin and he makes the rules for the house.'

'Yes, that's right.'

'Miss Dickson, what'll we do while the girls hog the bath?'

'Good point. First, while I'm here playing this game, you can call me Angie, and I'll call all of you Private. Second, all the privates not having a bath now will help me gather the clothes that are scattered all over the floor.'

'Hey, Angie, that sounds like work to me.'

'No. The enemy could be using that as excellent hiding places.'

'Really?'

'Too right. We'll start here. Put them in piles of the same colour to start with.'

In no time at all the lounge room once again had a floor instead of wall-to-wall clothing. Squeals of delight were coming from the bathroom, as the girls played in the bubbles and washed each other's hair. Angie had anchored the toddlers in a blocked off corner where they were amusing themselves with some toys. Was there really a sink in the kitchen or had it been taken over by aliens that resembled pizza boxes, chip containers and so many glasses? You'd have thought everyone in the building drank here. Soon there were bundles of squashed and tied up pieces of cardboard lined up in military precision. The glasses were once again shining and cleared away to the cupboard. Now, Angie thought, was a good time to have a changing of the guard in the bath. This wasn't real easy, as the girls were having a great time in the bath, but when shown their new uniforms and told of their next task, they were eager to please.

'Angie, are ya sure bubble baths are okay for boys? It won't make us … it won't turn us into sissies, will it?'

'Do the girls seem changed?'

'Ah, no, but they do smell kinda nice though.'

'Okay, men, who's ready to take the plunge? One word of warning, take care, if the enemy are lurking about in the bath, they hate bubbles. So you might need some assistance from your brothers to attack them.'

'Will the bubbles hurt, Angie?'

'No. I think the bubbles in a bubble bath feel like the big fluffy white clouds you see in the sky, during summer, and I haven't heard anyone say they've been hurt by them, have you?'

'No, and I've seen birds fly through them.'

'Private girls, line up for inspection. How do you feel, girls?'

'Angie, my skin feels all sort of tingly.'

'And my hair was squeaking all the time I was combing it.'

'That's great. I think maybe you've beaten some of the enemy already.'

'You said we're going to help make soup, but why? Mam just opens some cans. Can't you do that?'

'Yes I can, but we're on our island and there are no shops, only gardens. So, we can't buy cans of soup.'

'Oh! But how can gardens make soup?'

'No, no, not the gardens, but what grows in the garden.'

'Really? You mean flowers and daisies and grass?'

'Oh dear. I'd best start at the beginning and explain it properly.'

So Angie sat down on the floor with the girls and went through the basic details of how people cook their own soup.

'First, I'll put the boiler of soup stock that I brought with me on the stove to warm it up a bit. As we are going to make chicken vegetable soup, it has chicken bones I've already boiled up, then removed the bones and cut up the chicken meat.'

All eyes were as big as saucers; in fact, Angie felt a bit like a famous magician casting spells on the unwary.

'Now, you two can start peeling the carrots, okay?

'But Angie, we don't know how.'

After a few quick lessons and explanations about the vegies Angie had brought, the children were more than happy with their own little jobs towards making the soup. By the time the two other helpers from the Women's Centre had arrived, clothes were soon soaking, washing and drying on the clothes-horse. Beds had been attacked, stripped and surrendered to a powerful burst of cleanliness. Someone had had the presence of mind to bring a couple of oil burners and some perfumed oils. Soon there was a chorus of, 'What smells nice? It smells like flowers. When will the soup be ready? Can I stir this time? Can I try it yet?'

'Okay troops, line up 'til I can see we haven't thrown anyone out with the rubbish. One, two, three, four, five … No, everyone's still here.'

Angie sat back and surveyed what had been achieved as the children all tucked into their very own homemade soup and crusty bread. She thought, *Now if only we can get them to bed and asleep without too much trouble.* There was really no need to worry as they'd all worked so hard, helping with everything they were quite willing and even ready for bed.

Angie Dickson was extremely pleased with how things had worked out at the Sims' household, so much so that she was asleep when her head hit the pillow. She also hoped that Mrs Sims would not take what she had achieved as a sleight against her way of keeping house. If she was willing, Angie had made up her mind she was more than prepared to offer some assistance until the new babies had grown into a routine. It would work out well because she had only been relief teaching and that had come to an end with the return from long-service of the permanent grade three teacher, and she really needed some hands on experience for her social work degree that was coming together nicely.

'Angie, Angieeeeeee … You awake?' Suzy prodded with one icy cold hand. 'I was wondering about Liam and Mam, they're not dead are they?'

'Suzy, dear, of course not, why on earth would you think that? Your mum has gone to see Liam, who by the way is feeling a lot better, and while she was there at the hospital the new babies decided it was time they were born.'

'But … a long time ago, me great grandfather went to hospital and he never, *never* came home again. Me da said it's true, really.'

Chapter 14

Mrs Sims and Mrs Brown were getting on like two old friends sitting there together at the hospital; neither had wanted to leave before Liam returned from the theatre. In fact, Di Brown really had to admit to herself she may have been a little too harsh in judging Liam's mum as lazy and uncaring.

'Mrs. Sims, are you sure you don't want to go round to the maternity ward yet?'

'Suppose I should, but I've got to see Liam is all right first. Oh oo … Mmm … That was a powerful one. I think they're getting impatient.'

'Could I at least tell the staff to get in contact with Mr Sims? He should be here for moral support, if nothing else. I'm sure he would offer encouragement when the time is close.'

'No, not my Ronnie, he won't come into the hospital. Says it's got something to do with his grandfather getting a rough deal when he was a younger man. Must have been real bad 'cause Ronnie won't even talk about it. Once when I had the courage I asked his father. He blew up like a fire cracker, so I know he won't come.'

'Here, let me rub your back for you. I can still remember how mine ached during the birth of my children.'

'Oh that's good, thanks very much. Mrs Brown ... on the subject of backs ...'

'Here we are Sims. I told you your fan club would still be waiting for your return, but no, you wouldn't believe anything I told you!'

'Oh, Mam ... Mrs Brown, I was ...'

'Aaaarrh, ooo ... I've got to go. I can't wait any longer.'

'Mam ... Mam ... What's the ... mat—'

That was all Liam managed to say before he drifted back to sleep.

'Don't worry, Liam. It's just time for the babies to be born and sometimes they get a bit impatient and try to rush,' said Mrs Brown quietly, not really knowing if he could hear her, but she felt as though it was reassuring to him. 'Your mum will be busy and you must sleep. I promise we'll go as soon as the doctors say it's okay for you to see the new babies.'

'Where's Dilly?'

'His nana had to take him home; they waited with us until it got quite late. You'll see him in the morning.'

'You mean it's night already!'

'Yes Liam, you've been asleep for quite a while in recovery, but you need more sleep now.'

chapter 15

Ronald Sims had not returned home that night, which was really nothing new, because sometimes he was called to work on an urgent job that just couldn't wait for normal working hours. But he already knew of Liam's accident and his wife going into labour, through a well-informed network of eyes and ears that could have been likened to the fabled bush telegraph. His thoughts had dwelled fleetingly on the other children who would perhaps be alone in their unit, but no, informants had reassured him that there was a couple of females spending time with his kids. *Good*, he thought. *I think I'll tell Angelo I'm bunking down at his place until Leila comes home.* It would be a bit embarrassing to have strangers residing with him and the kids. Who knows, he could make a few dollars on the side, extra that Leila wouldn't know about. It always seemed to Ronnie that he could never put a dollar or two away for a rainy day because it seemed Leila always thought it was a rainy day. She had been a real brainbox of a chick, but when it came to running a budget for the house, she was, in Ronnie's mind, an utter moron.

Now Ronnie's mind was racing back to that magical summer that he and Leila shared. She had seemed so grown-up and knew everything about anything, but he now knew it had all been a great bluff. Leila only knew about schoolwork from books. She had never had to work. She had never even learnt to cook. And hadn't he made life even harder for himself when he had treated her like his princess. Sure, she loved it when he told her to go and lie down for a while. Somehow he would manage to put a meal together and do the washing at the same time. Then after Liam's birth, she had just seemed to give up altogether, except for producing babies nearly once a year. Ronnie could still remember how she had lashed out in uncontrolled anger when he brought up the subject of birth control. The fear of unnatural birth control came from ingrained teaching of the church that it was a terrible sin against God to use any form of unnatural birth control. Ronnie loved his children but it would have been a much easier life if they'd only had two or three.

Hey there, Ronnie boy, you know you wouldn't change a damn thing. You'd be totally lost without Leila, said that little voice inside his head as it shook away all the dreamy thoughts and brought him back with a thud to the real, dirty and cruel world that he was now part of.

'Hey Angelo. I've never asked for favours, but …'

'No, Ronnie baby, there's no credit without the goods.'

A somewhat stunned Ronnie replied, 'Geez, mate. I was going to ask if I could bunk down with you, just until Leila comes home.'

'Oh man, sometimes my mouth just runs wild,' Angelo said as he slapped Ronnie on the back.

'It's okay Angelo, suppose I should have said it differently or something …'

'I'd love to have you stay Ronnie. Will you be looking for a bit of extra work, with top dollar payment for my best mate?'

'Yeah, but nothing rough. I don't want no trouble with the cops.'

'Would I ever put you in a bad situation? Would I, Ronnie? Haven't I always managed to keep the cops away? Even when they come asking all those loaded questions?'

Ronnie thought quietly about the numerous close shaves he'd had lately with Angelo's deliveries, that he knew in his own mind that they were quite certainly drugs.

'Too right, mate. Dunno what I was thinking.'

'Would you maybe fancy a change of scenery for a couple of days? There's an interstate freighter that I know is short of an off-sider who knows the ropes. Are you interested?'

'Sure thing, but I don't have a heavy rigid endorsement on my licence, and which way is it going and for how long?'

'Hey hey, what's with all the questions?'

'Sorry, mate. That's none of my business.'

'No sweat. You'll have all the necessary papers delivered to you when you meet the driver of the freighter. By the way, I think I'd pack light clothes.'

'Thanks, Angelo. You're a real mate, you really are.'

'Um, just one thing, Ronnie. If there's any trouble, and I mean anything, I don't want any mention of my involvement. Just think of your kids when and if you feel like talking.'

'That's cool. Never knew you anyway,' Ronnie replied as his brain was flashing danger signals, but it was too late now. There'd be no backing away from Angelo.

With the details now etching themselves into his brain, there was nothing else he could do but throw a couple of clothes together that he got at the op-shop, pick up a toothbrush and razor from the shop on the corner and make his way to the warehouse where he was to meet with the driver. One thing Ronnie hadn't counted on was questions – the fella who ran the local shop was never very chatty, but his brother was helping out today. Talk about being like chalk and cheese. His brother started nosing around asking all sorts of questions. Why did he have to be helping here today of all days? This incident was just one more that had gone wrong today in Ronnie's thinking. He was almost ready to return to Angelo's pizza shop and say he'd changed his mind. Then Ronnie remembered Angelo's last warning to him, 'Just think about your kids'. He'd never be allowed to walk away from this job now. Ronnie answered the questions with snappy answers that should have warned the fella it could be dangerous to know too much. But the fella's imagination was on fire. He had watched all the police dramas on TV and his brother-in-law was a detective trying to break-up a vicious drug trade gang that had started up in the area.

Chapter 16

Dylan was up quite early. In fact, his grandparents were both still sound asleep, and so they didn't hear his fussing about in the kitchen. *Nana will really be surprised when she sees that I've prepared breakfast for her and Grandy,* thought Dylan as he busied himself with the porridge, toast and poached eggs. When he had prepared everything ready for cooking, he got out the tablecloth from the drawer and began to set the table for the three of them. He then thought it would be nice to put a couple of fresh flowers in a vase. Whilst hunting through the cupboard in the back porch for a vase, he saw Grandy's photo album that he used for family history. All thoughts of the vase suddenly flew from his mind as his hand travelled over the open page. He was amazed to see Grandy had a photo of Liam. But what was Liam doing in the country holding that horse? Grandy had an area designed on the back veranda where he could spread out his family history work and not have to pack it up at the end of each day. His current branch of the tree was headed up on the magnetic white board, and it was here that a copy of the black and white picture again now held Dylan's attention. He'd spent hours sitting out here in the warm comfort with Grandy when he'd first come out of hospital. Only then Dylan was consumed with so much self anger at the world, he didn't take any interest in what Grandy was showing him or even when he was telling him about years of history and intrigue that was woven into the Hunter family tree. Dylan was shocked by what he saw, so much that he felt frozen in time. Then his mind started with one hundred and one questions.

Where did Grandy get that photo? Was it one of those trick ones, where you just have your head showing with a different body? But the house in the background, it was too true to be a trick, but the horse was very different, so were the clothes. How and when had the photo been taken and why didn't anyone tell him about the secret visit? Or was it just, once again, everyone trying to protect him from how he might feel about things?

Dylan was still in the same spot with his walking frame parked like an illegal vehicle in a no-standing zone. The thoughtfully chosen flowers were now beginning to look bedraggled and slightly past their use-by date. Grandy could not understand the sight that met him as he approached the back door. Whatever could have upset Dylan? Or had he hurt his back somehow? It was at this same moment Dylan realised he was no longer alone and he turned so quickly it made him wince loudly with pain.

'Grandy. Why didn't you tell me? Why not ... that you knew Liam all the time?'

'Good morning to you too, Dylan.'

'BUT GRANDY!' Tears were now beginning to form. 'When did Liam visit with Mum and Dad? Why does everyone keep secrets from me? It's just not fair how you all think that I need protection from the truth.' Now tears were overflowing and Dylan had begun sobbing his heart out.

'Marie, Marie, quickly. Come here quick.'

'It's okay, Dylan, really it is, but I have no idea what you're talking about.'

This had no effect, in fact, it seemed to upset the boy even more. *Where, oh where is that woman when she's needed?* On hearing all the commotion, Marie was still trying to get her dressing gown on as she hurried out to the veranda.

'Dylan, there, there, it's alright. Whatever has happened, it can't be that bad.'

John Hunter knew instantly things would be all right. Thank goodness Marie always had a cool head, although he still marvelled about how she did it. How she always knew just what to say and what to do. *Must be one of those woman things,* he thought. *Now's a good time to go down the street and buy the paper. Let Marie do her magic on calming the boy down.*

'Nana. I hate it. I really do. I HATE IT.'

'Dylan, whatever is it? What's got you so worked up today?'

'Nana, please don't. Don't you do it too!'

'What? What am I doing dear?'

'Oh, Nana, don't. I thought you were the one person in all the world that I could trust always.'

'But you can dear, of course you can, Dylan. Talk to me, tell me what the trouble is?'

'WHY? Why didn't you tell me before?' Then Dylan was once again consumed with a flood of anguish that unleashed torrents of tears and his body was racked with such bone shuddering sobs that even Marie had trouble dealing with his torment.

'Dylan, darling. Now you are starting to worry me as well as your grandfather.'

'Yes, b-b-but ... it's his ... it's ... it's his fault.'

'Dylan, whatever has happened? If you can't tell me, I'll never be able to help you. Please start at the beginning and I promise I'll listen very carefully.'

As they looked at each other, instantly they knew the first and most important thing was to give and receive a Nana hug. It always lessened the hurt and, more importantly, it silently told each other, *No matter what, I'll always love you.*

'Nana, please come out to Grandy's desk.'

'But, we can talk here …'

The stony look told Marie already she was not listening to exactly what the child was trying to explain.

'Sorry, Dylan.'

Marie then walked silently behind Dylan, but in her head she could hear the same old argument: *Why did that dreadful accident put a beautiful boy like this in that hideous contraption he now uses to get about with?*

'There it is! Why couldn't even you tell me about it? I've always trusted you, Nana. Why didn't you say he'd been to my home? He even told me he'd never been near a horse. But there, Grandy's got a photo of him. No wonder you were so concerned for him when we were at the hospital.'

'Hold on, Dylan. Hold it right there. I still don't know what you're talking about. Who is this "he" that you're so angry about? And who's been to your home? And what horse are you talking about?'

Dylan had never lost his temper in front of Nana before, but now he was thumping his fists on the desk and his face was reddening by the minute. Dylan heard the side gate and figured Grandy was now home again. So he turned ready to face him full-on as he came through the door.

'Grandy. How could you keep it from me all this time?'

John looked at Marie for a clue but found none, only more confusion than he had.

'I don't know what it's all about, John. But he's very angry about someone, a horse and someone going to his home!'

'Here, Grandy. HERE'S THE PROOF! Why couldn't you tell me? Why did you let me think he'd made friends with me because he liked me? Did you have to pay him very much? I know he does favours for people. WHY, GRANDY, WHY?'

Before John and Marie had time to put two and two together, Dylan was off into his room with a slam of the door that felt as though an earthquake had just hit the house.

'Marie, what does he mean, "here's the proof"? Who did I pay and for what favours?'

Marie bent down to pick up the photo that seemed to be the cause of Dylan's anger, although she couldn't think why.

'Marie, what is it? Are you all right, dear? Sit, sit down here.'

She was now beginning to grasp some of what had just been going on.

'What happened, dear? Here, have a sip of water. Should I ring the doctor? You look awful. I've a good mind to go and deal with Dylan now. I thought you were going to pass out.'

'Yes, so did I! You've not met his best mate from school yet, have you?'

'No. It was going to be this next weekend, if he hadn't been hurt at school.'

'That's right. But this picture on your desk is a photo of whom? No … I'll tell you what Dylan thinks. I'm sure of that now. He thinks that this is *Liam*. If you look carefully you will see the building behind that person. It's your grandfathers home, which is also now Dylan's home.'

'Well, blow me! Evidently, you never met this person. If my charts serve me correctly, that would be young Ronald Simmonds. He was my second cousin, even distantly related to your family too. History says he died in hospital when he was a young man of about twenty-one, I think. You know, I'd forgotten all about him. He was Uncle Harry's boy. Quite a bit of a tearaway, always seemed to follow trouble around or maybe it followed him. But I still don't see why a picture of my cousin and his horse taken at Grandfather's place would be the cause of Dylan's temper tantrum this morning. You really must be firmer with the boy. He has to know what is expected of him when he is in our home and we're responsible for him.'

'Yes, but …'

'No, dear. I mean it: you must be firmer. It'll be for his own good in the long run.'

'Yes, but Dylan thinks that is a picture of *Liam*.'

'Now, why on earth would he think that? Why would I have a photo of his best friend, whom so far, I have not even met or seen? Now really dear, I just can't see where that reasoning is coming from. Can't you see that maybe Dylan suffered more than just back and leg injuries in the accident?'

'JOHN. You take that thought back. How can you even think that?'

With that the couple each went about doing various things alone and silently. It was a very eerie silence that had now descended on the home where three people were building personal barriers that, if action wasn't taken soon, would become an impregnable obstacle to remove. Even the breakfast setting sat forlornly, unused after Dylan's surprise meal didn't eventuate.

Chapter 17

'**G**'day mate, the name's Ron. Ron S—'

'Don't want to know what your name is, stupid. If the coppers ever ask, I can say I've no idea who you are. Just some hitchhiker looking for a ride instead of walking in the weather.'

'Oh yeah. Sorry. I didn't think.'

'That's right, mate. You fellas never think. I can't see the connection you all have with Angelo.'

'Angelo, he's a—'

'You sure don't learn too quick, do ya?'

'Oh yeah. I feel quite tired, think I'll have forty winks. Then I won't be saying anything else that you don't want to hear.'

'Now you've caught on, mate. I'll wake you when it's your shift at handling this beauty.'

Ronnie really had no intention of going to sleep in the company of this man who was driving this magnificent vehicle with a covered trailer to match. He sat quietly. It had been fortunate that he'd thought to accidently borrow that pair of sunglasses whilst purchasing his necessities for this trip.

It really irritated him, how easy these days a person could borrow from shops, whether they were large complexes in a shopping centre or a family run corner store.

Now he began to study the interior of the truck that seemed more like an aerial navigation centre of a jet liner. However was he going to do his share of the driving? Hadn't he insisted to Angelo that he'd never driven anything bigger than his friends' four-wheel drive? They started to descend a long steep decline. Ronnie watched with child-like fascination as the truck engine took on a life of its own, screaming obscenities as its gears were changed down to a lower ratio to hold the speed without risk of burning out the brakes. Now, as the road levelled out again, the engine showed life by letting out a loud audible sigh. Maybe it was grateful for no longer having the weight of its trailer pushing unmercifully against the loaded truck body. Ronnie was thinking how unusually peaceful it was sitting high up in this high-tech cabin as the towns quickly disappeared behind the cloud of dust that was their faithful companion. Ronnie had adapted quickly to the *sleep-when-you-can* lifestyle at the truck pull-ins and rushed meals at the roadside cafes. The landscape was now nothing more than the occasional clump of trees, a lonely roadside mailbox that showed the start of a two-wheel rut roadway that would eventually lead to a homestead. The truck made a sudden lurch to the other side of the road, which caused Ronnie to be thrown hard against the door, making him cry out in alarm.

'Damn, blast those buffalo. Stupidest animals I've ever known on a road. They're a real menace.'

'Oh. Whose are they? Have they trampled a fence down somewhere?' asked Ronnie in a somewhat shaken voice as he rubbed his shoulder that had taken the full force of hitting the window and the door.

'Geez. Where on earth does Angelo get you guys from? Don't you know anything? Have you never ventured any further from the city than the outer suburbs? No, don't tell me. I really don't need to know anything.'

With that sudden outburst he quickly settled back into the silent mood of driving, calmly adjusting the state of the truck back to its own allotted space and speed on the road. However the tranquillity of the cabin was then shattered with the static squawking of the radio positioned just above the sun-visor on the driver's side.

'Okay, Ronnie boy, in about one hundred or so kilometres, we're going to meet up with the first of our deliveries as well as pass on some of our cargo.'

'Great. When we've unloaded, give me a few minutes to grab some food. I'm starving.'

'Ronnie boy, if you look in the sleeper you'll see that I restocked the fridge at the last cafe. Just take out whatever you want. I'll have a Mars bar and a cold can.'

'Yeah, but … I need some more gum. You see, I'm trying hard to toss the cigs.'

'Well, you'll have to settle for whatever is in the back. You'll be lucky if you get to meet two blowflies at the changeover stop.'

'What sort of town are we stopping at?'

'You know, you ask too many questions. Who said anything about it being a town, Ronnie boy? We will stop wherever the plane can put down.'

As Ronnie leaned over and began scrutinising the contents of the fridge, the conversation of the last five minutes was being replayed inside his head.

Hell and damnation Leila, what have I done this time! he thought silently. It wasn't until Ronnie was back sitting in the truck's cabin that the full impact of what he was now becoming involved with suddenly hit him. His brain was working overtime as he was now able to fit the pieces together. No wonder Angelo was such a generous, fun-loving guy that seemed to have a neverending supply of friends. In hindsight, Ronnie remembered it was Angelo's lifestyle of having a good time, plenty of mates and always seeming to have a spare dollar to share that had overridden the intuition he'd felt when he'd been offered a couple of jobs that had paid really well. Ronnie's thoughts were now with Leila, the girl he'd loved since, well, since forever. Pain rose in his chest making it hard to breath. Now tears welled in his eyes as his mind was saying, *I love you. I love you so much it hurts. God Leila, what have I done this time?*

'Hey there, Ronnie boy, what's the matter? You're not going to throw up or anything, are you? You're forgetting about your duty. Remember, you're supposed to be looking for the plane.'

'Yeah mate, but I wish the thing would just drop out of the sky and disappear forever.'

'Hey. Don't encourage tragedy. The pilot is a mate of mine. Together we've done nearly twenty-five quick drop jobs in this area, without any suspicion at all. So, just shut up and keep looking, Ronnie boy.'

'Air one to road doggie, air one to—'

'Okay already. You really don't have to advertise our position to the entire dead heart.'

'Gee, who got out on the wrong side this morning?'

'Shut it. Just give us your location. If you're real lucky we might even decide to meet you.'

'We? You mean you haven't ditched that new off-sider yet? Slack mate, that's all I can say. SLACK."

Instantaneously, two pairs of eyes were scanning the sky when unexpectedly there was a great roar that seemed to be almost on the cabin roof.

'Blasted fool. I'll tell him what for.'

All that was visible from the truck was swirling red dust. In fact, their world had now become a choking, oppressive and seething redness that was invading everything in its path.

'Damn fool. Hold on, Ronnie boy.'

The truck now took on a life of its own, weaving from side to side and the engine began to cough and splatter. Its two captives held on for dear life, as they tried to regain control of the massive mechanical monster. As it cautiously began to slow, Ronnie saw the plane gracefully gliding to earth, just as a leaf does in a gentle breeze.

'That fool could have killed both of us. One day his practical jokes will be the death of him. Just you wait and see.'

'Yeah. Okay, whatever. But we're fine now,' said Ronnie as he tried to rearrange his clothing that was now sticking to him closer than a second skin.

By now the plane was sitting quietly, though dust was still swirling as the propellers kept rhythm with each other whilst awaiting the kick that would send them soaring once again. Once the truck's engine had eased back to a gentle idle instead of its thunderous roar, the cabin door flew open.

'What the hell were—?'

'Save it, mate, time is precious and I've got places to be in a hurry, like before yesterday.'

Ronnie thought it best if he stayed put in the cabin of the truck, maybe because he had a horrible thought that if he tried to stand, he might collapse because instead of legs he felt as though he had two lengths of not quite set jelly. There seemed to be a swarm of bees in his head, each waving a dazzling light that was swimming before his eyes. Reality tried to return to normal as Ronnie heard loud slamming of metal doors together with obscenities being yelled back and forth. Ronnie increased the volume of the current CD. After a while, he thought he should maybe go and help or just see what was happening, but just as his fingers gripped the release handle, there was a deafening roar of an engine being pushed to its limits a little too quickly. Ronnie turned in the direction of the noise, the red clouds once again enveloped the truck, obliterating everything but the view of the interior of the mighty truck cabin. Time itself was racing on but at the same time it was briefly trapped inside with Ronnie as he sat lost within the thoughts racing inside his head. With a jolt, Ronnie suddenly had a feeling something was not quite right, but what? Then it struck him: it was too, too quiet. Where was his tormentor? The truck was still idling away, much like a contented cat purring, but where was that maniac that Angelo employed to drive this thing? Gently, he eased the door open, not knowing what was awaiting him. Ronnie had never experienced the fear that was consuming him right now, but raw instinct was driving him. He had to face whatever demon was waiting.

Chapter 18

Liam woke with a start when someone's call button alerted more than just the nursing staff. It took him quite a few minutes before he could recall the events of the last two days. Then, when only a quick shift of his body in the bed brought a scream of pain, he knew it hadn't been a dream. Suddenly, there was a nurse holding his hand with a touch so gentle Liam wondered if she was one of the spirit angels his mam often talked about. With the thoughts of Mam, tears began filling his eyes 'til they overflowed, flooding his face and chest. This brought anxiety and concern from the young nurse, who had almost finished her first attempt at working nights.

'Oh dear, is your arm hurting that much, Liam? By looking at your chart, I could give you some more medication that would help you.'

'I'm okay. It hurts a bit, but I was really thinking about Mam.'

'Mam … Oh you mean your mother.'

'Yes. How is she? Is she okay? When she was with Dilly and Mrs Brown she didn't look so good. Can I see her now, can I?'

'No, it wouldn't be such a good idea right now.'

'Why? She's dead, isn't she? I just knew something bad was gunna happen. I just knew it.'

With that, Liam was once again caught up in his own flood of tears that he no longer had any sort of control over. But it wasn't hurt that was causing them. He, like most young boys (even tough ones), needed his mother's arms and soothing words when he was troubled. Upon hearing all the commotion, the night duty supervisor, Carol, came in to check on her latest graduate nurse Emma. Carol beckoned Emma to the door of the room so that she could try and work out who needed help first; Emma, who was looking bewildered and unsure of herself in the face of so many tears; or Liam, who was sobbing his heart out.

'I don't know Carol, for some reason he thinks his mother has died. Nothing I've said or done has calmed him down.'

'It's all right, Emma. There's a notation on his papers that his mum went to the labour ward at the same time he was coming back to the children's ward. Perhaps his thoughts are a little jumbled after the anaesthetic.'

'I'll give maternity a quick call and see what they can tell us. What's his name? Oh yes, Sims. I won't be a minute.'

Meanwhile in the labour ward, Leila herself was worried. *I've never had this much trouble before*, she thought. It was at this moment the doctor who was in charge came and examined Leila again. The worry that showed on his tired face was infectious.

'Sorry about this, Mrs Sims, but if we don't operate soon, we may lose you as well as your twins.'

He was totally unprepared for the look of absolute horror that took a fleeting dance across Leila's already exhausted, tear-stained face.

'Mrs Sims. It's okay, Mrs Sims we have things in control, but we really need to do something about your twins. The staff have been trying to contact Mr Sims, but so far we've been unable to find him.'

'Thanks, doctor, but if it's just a signature on the consent form, it's okay I'll sign it now. You'd never get my Ronnie coming in here, especially now that there's a hint of trouble.'

'Alright, Mrs Sims, and thank you. We'd best start getting things moving, quickly.'

The staff at once began to resemble a frenzy caused by panic, only there was the absence of real panic, just trained people doing what they do best. In what seemed like no time at all, Leila was being wheeled into the prepared theatre. By now, the staff had gained an insight into the terror Leila had about not having her babies naturally. It all stemmed from her island culture, which was still strongly ingrained into the very fibre of her being. So Leila was only given enough anaesthetic to calm her completely. Then an epidural was given, to deaden the lower parts of her body, before the doctor proceeded with the caesarean birth. There was an unnatural spark of concern between the staff around the table once the two beautiful babies had been successfully delivered.

'Mrs Sims, can you hear me? You've seen and held your beautiful twins, but now I really need to put you to sleep for a short time. Just while we tidy things up and put things back in order for you.'

'Um … ah … um. Whatever.'

Thankfully, Leila was now totally oblivious to the anxiety that now filled the operating theatre. Trays of instruments were appearing as if by magic, not to mention the increase of medical staff.

Dr Paul Hill was anxiously trying to plan how to attempt the next unexpected part of the surgery. He wished that his friend and fellow surgeon Doctor Lucas would hurry and arrive to assist in the complicated operation that was to come.

'Is Doctor Lucas here yet, nurse?'

'Yes, Paul. I've just finished scrubbing up. What's the big excitement that caused you to demand my attention at this ungodly hour of the night?'

'The patient, Mrs Leila Sims. We've just done a C-section and delivered two beautiful babies.'

'Yes, well that's lovely, Paul, but—'

'Well, just take a look at the size of the growth that's here. I really thought we'd miscalculated about the number of babies we were to deliver.'

'Mmm … See what you mean, old man. Did she mention any concerns during the pregnancy, anything that was different?' asked Dr Paul Hill.

'Not that I know of, only for quite a time now she's been feeling unwell and hasn't had much of an appetite. I mistakenly thought it was just the stress of carrying the twins along with the added pressure from her other children at home. Also, I thought it couldn't hurt if she lost weight through loss of appetite. She's really been doing it tough for quite a few months now.'

'Yes, she has. Paul, she's a very lucky woman. If she had had those babies naturally, as she wanted, she wouldn't have lived. You've done an excellent job here tonight. Make sure the lab checks the outcome of this growth.'

Leila was sleeping peacefully in the high dependency unit, unaware of the drama that had played out after the birth of her beautiful twins. Both doctors, Paul Hill and Tom Lucas, were still at the hospital, not expecting any more drama, catching up with each other. They had been friends since primary school until they each branched into their own fields of medicine. Tom had gone into surgery, whilst Paul had favoured gynaecology.

'That patient of yours, Mrs Sims, really had things stacked against her during her pregnancy. I don't envy you at all in having to explain that there will be no more little Sims.'

'Yeah. That I feel will have to be delivered with great diplomacy.' Paul sighed, already dreading the impending chat he'd soon have to have with his patient.

'Amen to that. But it's not like she hasn't already exceeded the average number of off-spring that most families receive.'

Stifling a yawn, Paul was quick to jump to the defence of Mrs Sims. 'Yes, but if the world had just a handful of truly devoted parents like her, it would be a much better place for today's children to grow up in.'

'Steady on, mate, point taken.' The anxiety showed in Tom Lucas's voice a little too strongly.

Tom now realised he'd probably over-stepped the mark of friendship with his remarks about Mrs Sims.

'What have you got planned for next Wednesday afternoon? Thought it would be nice to get together, away from all this.'

'Hey, that's a good idea, Tom. How about I meet you at the squash centre? That is, if you can stand taking a beating.'

A voice through the PA system announced that Dr Paul Hill was needed in the labour ward, ending the conversation.

Chapter 19

'Liam dear, I've just spoken to the maternity ward, and your mum is doing just fine. She's a little tired at the moment, so you can't go and see her right now.'

Liam was conjuring up all sorts of images in his mind, but this quickly vanished as the night sister held out her arms as he began to crumble. For a tough little cookie he was sure learning fast that not all adults were out to get a kid. In fact, he was finding it extremely comforting to receive a cuddle when he felt as though his world was collapsing all around him. When his sobbing had eased to hiccups and shudders he tried to let his newfound ally know that he understood, but now he was also in a lot of pain.

'No worries, Liam. Of course I can do something to ease that for you.'

After she'd settled Liam down again, she dragged out his file to notate the medication, but also, more importantly, she attached a sticky note to the front that asked the morning staff to ensure that Liam was taken to the nursery first thing to see his new baby siblings. The rest of the shift, for the night staff, passed quickly with no interruptions. The one exception was in the mind of Sister Jill Evans. She was reminiscing of the time long ago when she too had given birth to twins. It was hard thinking how they had now both gone their own ways in the world. In fact, to the opposite ends of the world. David and Bruce had never really been that close, unlike most twins. However with the premature death of their father, during that stupid politically bungled drug bust, they had both had to age more quickly than their young years. Like mothers the world over, Jill still caught herself thinking of her strapping young men of twenty-five as her boys. *Where had all those years gone?* Of course, they would always be her precious little boys, but she would have to say something about their lack of communication. *I mean there's more to say than just 'happy birthday' or 'Merry Christmas.'* She was mentally placing a reminder in her brain that she would have to try harder when she next she wrote to them both.

Chapter 20

Angie was so grateful that she had brought her newly acquired mobile phone with her, but the only time she had privacy was to take it with her into the loo. Even then, there was always something or someone trying to demand attention. She'd told herself just two quick calls: one to Di Brown, and the other to the hospital. Not in a million years would she ever have dreamt the responses that she got from exchange of information:

Dylan's grandfather had a black and white photo of Liam at Dylan's home holding a horse. Although it wasn't really Liam, but a young second cousin of Mr Hunter that died in a fire at the age of twenty-two. Mrs Sims being so close to death and not knowing anything about the trouble she had suffered. It was strange that the time of the operation was the same time Angie was woken up by Suzy who was greatly distressed thinking her mother was dead.

The hairs on the back of Angie's neck were now all standing to attention. She could recall, years ago, some friends explaining about psychic experiences, but hadn't she dismissed those thoughts because really they'd just been a bit of fun and nonsense? Now, her brain was flat out trying to come up with a logical explanation of how Suzy knew at the precise time about her mother, and also why Liam, who didn't have close friends, had more or less taken Dylan under his wing. Angie told herself that when her life was back to normal she would contact David and Lynette and try to look rationally at the library of information they had on psychic research. All these thoughts were abruptly pushed aside by the screams and yells coming from the boys' bedroom.

'Boys. For goodness sake, open the door.'

As the words left her mouth, Angie realised teacher-mode was not the way to handle this situation. *Think Angie, think.* It was extremely hard to think when she could hear the yells of abuse and small bodies hitting objects in the room. What on earth had happened? A flash of inspiration crossed Angie's troubled brain.

'Battle emergency. Enemy presence alert. Attention all trained soldiers, form your battle lines now. Report NOW.'

Nothing happened for a moment but ever so slowly the ruckus coming from the closed door stopped. Quickly Angie returned to the lounge room and started rearranging a few objects. The three boys entered the room together, unsure of what to expect.

'Great, you're all still in one piece. I thought for a moment I was too late in sounding the alarm.'

The surprised look on all three boys was indescribable; Angie recovered to serious thinking by quickly checking her shoelaces before her laughter could escape.

'What's the matter Miss Dic—'

'He means, what do ya want, er … Angie?'

'Well, it's just that … Well, you know, I didn't want the three of you fighting the battle all on your own in there. Sometimes the unseen enemy can be really tricky. It can cause you to think you have to fight everybody, even when you are all on the one side.'

'Oh! That's real sneaky, Miss … Angie.'

'Are ya sure ya not tricking us, Angie?'

The older of the three boys decided he needed to step up and take the lead in Liam's absence. 'Geez, will you two pipe down? I think she really might know what was happening.'

'Great, great men, I knew you were all really clever. It's just sometimes the enemy gets, um … sneaky.'

By now, the boys had completely forgotten what their argument was about and were once again best mates. Angie thought, *If only life itself was as easy to rectify as I just achieved with these three.*

chapter 21

What Ronnie found at the rear of the truck made him keel over.

'What the hell … What'd he go and do that for?' came tumbling out of his mouth before he had time to think.

The driver – whatever his name was – was slumped against the rear wheels. Ronnie saw that no matter what help he could offer, it would make very little difference to the inevitable result. Decisions were racing back and forth at lightning speed within his brain. He chose not to move the driver but just tried to make him as comfortable as the situation would allow. Whilst he was getting some of the bedding from the cabin, inspiration came as the radio squawked. Ronnie then knew what he should have done half an hour before: radio for help from somewhere. *Police … mmm maybe, hospital … mmm possible, passing trucks – yes, but how?* Ronnie didn't know their call signs. Now, basic need took over, he picked up the receiver and said what jumped out from memories of action movies.

'May day, may day.'

Nothing happened. He tried again, this time by holding the black button in as he shouted his message again.

'May day, may day, please help me, someone. It's really bad. I need help please …'

Again nothing. Ronnie was still gripping the receiver so hard, he still had the transmit button engaged. He was just at the stage of giving up and going to check on the driver again as he replaced the receiver back in its cradle.

'Lone Tree Station here. Do you read? Lone Tree Station here. I may be able to assist, but not if you're a bleeding ship out here in the desert. Over.'

'Hello? Hello? Please help. Hello?'

'Take it easy, mate, okay? You have to calm down though if I'm going to be of any help.'

'Please, help. I think he's dying. Maybe he's already dead. I don't know what to do. Help me, for gawdsake, help me, please.'

By now, there was a third listener trying to break into the conversation. As Ronnie paused he jumped his chance.

'This is Sergeant Brothers, Territory Police. Can you give your location, may day caller?'

'Hi Sarge, Lone Tree here. He can't be too far from here, 'cause he's coming in crystal clear.'

'Yeah, thanks. May day, can you give your location?'

Hell and damnation, Ronnie thought. *The police arriving is the last thing I need.* But hell, the situation could not get any worse. So he tried his best in describing the landscape where the truck was parked. After what seemed an eternity sitting in the deathly quietness, Ronnie heard the noise of a small plane and immediately thought that the pilot had heard his message and was returning to either finish off the driver and himself, or to collect his delivery back, or perhaps both. The plane made its descent. Ronnie noticed it didn't come as close as previously, so that horrible red dust didn't cloud everything. As it ground to a stop, he saw the word 'doctor' written on the side. Relief began to feel really comfortable until he saw a second person alight from the plane. He was dressed in a police uniform.

Chapter 22

T he tension that consumed the Hunter household had eased slightly when the agreed visit to Liam was to go ahead. Marie had had to do a lot of soft talking to John just to get him to even think about still taking Dylan to the hospital. John had done what he thought was best, but just one look from Dylan defeated him.

'Okay, Dylan my man, what's wrong now?' asked Grandy

'Nothing. Well, nothing much, Grandy,' said Dylan.

'I give up. Marie, what have I done or not done now?' shouted Grandy.

'What's up, Dylan?' Marie asked quietly, 'We're ready to go.'

'It's Grandy. I'm not trying to be difficult, but could Grandy please wear his older shirt and jumper, perhaps even his gardening jeans?' pleaded Dylan.

'Boy oh boy, what gets into the heads of today's youth?'

'But, Dylan—'

'Think, Nana. What will Liam think if he sees Grandy dressed up in a shirt and tie? You know what he's like.'

'Well yes, Dylan. This time he's right, John. Liam will create barriers that wouldn't ever be broken with his first impression of you. It's only because he doesn't know you or love you yet, as we do. We already know you're a big cuddly pussycat.'

John walked back into the bedroom, shaking his head and muttering to himself. Marie had to admit to herself dressing down for Liam was something she had not thought of, but Dylan was probably right this time.

The car trip was tense and quiet. After leaving the car in the undercover carpark, they were walking towards the entrance of the hospital when it became obvious to Dylan that he'd have to say something to Grandy about how Liam might react.

'Yes, Dylan. I think I can understand how a kid like Liam might not have much time for us oldies.'

'He's really a great mate. It's just that a lot of adults seem to have treated him badly in the past.'

'Oh! Oh dear.' Marie gasped as she put her hand to the wall to steady herself.

'Dylan, would you mind terribly if we called into the kiosk first? I promise we won't take long, but I just need to sit down and have a drink.'

'Marie, what's wrong? You've gone very pale. I knew all this anger was no good.'

'No, John. No, it's just that I need to sit quietly and ask Dylan a couple of things.'

'What, Nana? What do you want?'

'Here's a table. How about you and Grandy share a chocolate milkshake? John we'll sit here while you go and get it, okay?'

The kiosk was thankfully not very busy, just a few hospital staff grabbing a quick snack.

'Dylan. I've been racking my brain trying to come up with a gentle way to approach this subject, but I can't.'

'Geez Nana, what's wrong?'

'It's about Liam. What you said before about adults treating him badly.'

'Aw, that's nothing, Nana.'

'No Dylan, you're wrong. While Mrs Brown was with him at the hospital, before the doctor saw him, his gown sort of came undone and … well, he has some rather nasty scars on his back. Do you know anything? Because Mrs Brown and the doctor are very concerned about what's been happening to him.'

John heard the conversation as he returned to the table. 'Yes Dylan, sounds as though Liam could do with some people being concerned.' He put the milkshake and two glasses and straws down in front of Dylan.

Dylan sat looking into his shake, deeply lost in his own private thoughts.

'You know, I bet it's got something to do with that big boy that's been hanging around school. Liam's always a bit jumpy when he's about. Miss Dickson ordered him out of the school grounds one day. That sure pumped Liam up. Now, what's the name Liam called him? Yes, that's it, Hilly. Silly Hilly. But I don't know anything about him and by what he looks like I don't want to either.'

'Is that what's got you so churned up and worried, Marie my love?'

'Yes, John. But let's not mention the subject unless Liam brings it up and that seems highly unlikely.'

Dylan knew before asking which room Liam was in. He had a way about him that attracted noise and loudness.

'Nana, Grandy, can I go in first, please? Just so I can tell him you're out here and that I'd like you to meet him?'

'Good thinking, my man. I'm sure Nana would appreciate having a quiet word or two with the duty sister, right Marie?'

Chapter 23

During working hours, Angie found looking after her little Sims charges, with the help of two assistants from the women's shelter, much easier than she had first anticipated. The real test would come this morning because she'd pre-arranged with the two helpers for a couple hours of freedom. A visit to Mrs Sims was needed, plus she'd like to see how Liam was getting on.

'Where ya goin Miss … er … Angie?' said one of the kids. 'No, ya can't leave us, no one'll be 'ere wif us!'

Now, Angie thought, *how do I wriggle out of this predicament without undoing all the trust and understanding the children have accepted?*

'Suzy, could you manage to help me quieten the rest of the troops? Then I'll try and explain the mission I must undertake. It could be very dangerous.'

'Hey, you lot – SHUD-UP! Angie's gonna tell us something if ya all be quiet.'

'Thanks, Suzy. My two helpers will be here shortly and they're going to be in charge for a couple of hours, okay?"

'Aw, Angie. We want ya to stay. Nobody's ever stayed with us before. It's always Liam who takes care of us. Where is he?"

Now there were screams and yells going again at an even louder volume than before. Mixed in with the children's noise was a very loud thumping on one of the adjoining walls of the unit, followed almost instantaneously with an equally loud knocking at the door. But Angie had guessed, or at least hoped she'd guessed rightly, that it would be her two helpers.

Suzy screamed, 'Quick Angie hide. Don't let 'im in!'

'Who, Suzy? Who's at the door?'

'Bet it's old Blackie. He lives next door and sometimes he comes and shouts at Mam. One time he even pushed 'er, but Liam got real angry and said lots of really rude words. Mam said he wasn't ta agin, because they were really rude and it weren't nice.'

As Angie made her way to the door, her brave little troops scattered to various bedrooms and hiding places, leaving just the toddlers sitting on the floor because they weren't quick enough yet to get away.

'Hello Helen, hello Barbara. Welcome to 'camp bedlam,' said Angie as she opened the door to the two startled visitors.

'Look, Angie, we were talking on the way over here. I don't know if we can manage these kids without you. You have a magic gift or something with how you get these kids to respond to any task you ask.'

'No, it's not magic. It's just, well, sort of an understanding. You've got to work in childlike thinking, that's all. It's nothing special. For now, just go along with whatever direction the flow of conversation takes, as I explain to them why I've got to go out for a couple of hours.'

The three women now walked into the lounge room together.

'Oh! Did you remember to bring the extra supplies I asked for?'

'Yes, Angie. But what on earth are you going to do with all the flour, salt and food colouring?'

'You'll see. Just be patient.'

'Privates, all present yourselves quickly, front and centre. We have a major problem with the enemy. It's nothing too hard but I'll need all the help you can give.'

Now without hesitation all the children went and sat in a circle that included the toddlers on the lounge room floor. Angie had to concentrate very carefully on what she was telling them and tried not to look at the ring of serious little faces that were before her, in case her laughter escaped and broke the spell. *Maybe it is magic,* she thought.

'So, that's how it is troops, without your expert co-operation in this matter I'm afraid the enemy will probably take over this island. I haven't heard yet, in all my dealings with them, that they are very nice to prisoners.'

'Gee, really Angie?'

'I'll 'elp. I will, really.'

'Great, troops, but I need you all to follow the orders that Helen and Barbara give you, because I've put them in charge for a while.'

As Angie gathered a few things together in her backpack, the other two women wondered if it would really work. Neither of them had ever made coloured play dough before, but they had to admit it should keep the kids occupied.

Chapter 24

'John, dear, would you be a love and go back to the kiosk and get a bottle of soft drink and perhaps a block of chocolate? I know Dylan said no, but my feeling is it may work as an icebreaker when we meet Liam shortly. While you're there, I'll have a word or two at the nurses station.'

'Of course dear, just knew you were itching for a chinwag,' said John as he disappeared into the lift, leaving Marie with no chance of reply. Marie turned from the lifts and made her way to the nurses station with Dylan in tow. She approached the ward receptionist to introduce herself.

'Hello. I'm Mrs Hunter.'

'You must be Dylan's grandmother. We, the staff that is, were beginning to wonder about this Dylan character. That's all we've heard of since Liam arrived. In fact, we began to doubt his existence. We thought it was probably an imaginary friend.' The receptionist smiled at Dylan as she said this, making him clutch his hand and hide behind Marie, too shy to respond. Marie took Dylan's hand and squeezed gently to provide reassurance.

'Yes, it's really wonderful, the friendship those two have forged in a short time.'

As Sister Jill Evans had only called in to tidy up a couple of reports on patients, before taking holiday leave for a couple of weeks, she had not intended to join in with the conversation that was happening, but a niggling thought was irritating her.

'Excuse me, Mrs Hunter, I couldn't help overhearing. Would you mind giving me a few minutes of your time? I have just a few loose ends in regard to Liam Sims that you may be able to help me tidy up.'

'Well, er yes, of course,' Marie replied as she looked around a little nervously.

Seeing the slight look of concern and hesitation, Jill quickly suggested they use the vacant consulting room next door to the nurse's station. Then she added,

'Dylan, why don't you go on in and see Liam whilst your grandma and I have a chat. I need to make sure Liam is getting the best care he can, and your grandma might be able to give us some suggestions on how to help him the best.'

Dylan looked towards Marie, uncertain if he should go on alone to see Liam,

'Go on Dylan, you go and have a good chat first before Grandy and I come' Marie said whilst gently pushing Dylan towards Liam's room. Once Dylan was on his way, Marie left a quick note for John, so he'd know where she was if he returned before she'd finished talking with Jill. Then Jill and Marie entered the empty room and closed the door to ensure their privacy.

Dylan walked down the corridor looking for the right room number. As he found it, he entered the room and quietly greeted Liam,

'G'day Liam.'

'Hi ya, Dilly. Geez, I missed ya, I mean, er ... I've been so busy here. Ya know them nurses don't know what it's like, being stuck in bed all day.'

'How's your arm, Liam? Does it still hurt a lot?'

'Nah, don't at all now.'

'Here we are, Liam. Sorry I took a bit longer in bringing your pills back to ease your pain, but someone's drip needed changing,' the nurse stated as she came into the room.

The silence in the room was electrifying, but the nurse either didn't notice or thought it better not to say anything.

'I told ya. I don't need 'em.'

She quickly sized up the situation. 'Sorry Liam, but the doctor has insisted. You don't want to get me in trouble, do you?'

'Aw, guess not. Give 'em 'ere.'

When she'd left the room she wondered if the two boys would overcome the tension that now crowded the room.

'Pills. That is the hardest thing I found when I was in hospital. Sometimes I couldn't even swallow them.'

'Really, Dilly?'

'Yes. I think I hated them more than anything else.'

The next instant saw the pills disappear down Liam's neck, followed by such a flood of water that Liam emitted an oversized burp.

'Oh, Liam, do you mind!'

'Not much, Dilly. Can ya do a better one?'

'Mrs Hunter, I don't know where to begin.'

'Please, it's Marie, and I think maybe you're talking about the same concern that has Di Brown worried sick.'

'His teacher, yes. She brought it to the attention of the staff when she was waiting with him in casualty. Can you shed any light on the subject?'

'Well, no, not really. I don't know much, but Dylan, my grandson, said he thinks it may have something to do with some older child named Hill. Evidently he's been causing a bit of trouble for Liam, if that's at all possible.'

'Yes, I know what you mean. He's a livewire isn't he? If I'm not mistaken he is also very wary of adults – all adults.'

'He is, but then I think his loud mouth probably causes

most of his unwanted abuse.'

'Surely not his back though?'

'No, I feel that's an entirely different issue altogether.'

'I know there's a consensus among the staff that the police should become involved, but I'm not sure that that won't increase the trouble.'

Both women sat thinking and knowing that the cause just had to be found quickly for Liam's sake.

'So, you see, Liam, that's why I'd like you to meet Grandy and Nana.'

'Aw, I dunno. If yer thought they was up to somefink, and ya not knowing people like me. Ya know I don't trust 'em – adults, I mean. I dunno Dilly.'

Now Dylan looked very disappointed with his friend, so much so that Liam burst out laughing.

'Gotcha, Dilly.'

'Liam, that's not nice. I thought you meant it.'

'Well, I didn't. So yeah, let 'um come in. I'll 'ave a look but I probably won't like 'um.'

Dylan went to the door and beckoned his grandparents into Liam's room. John walked straight up to the bed, placed the chocolate and drink on the table and held out his hand. 'Put it there, mate. I've waited a long time to finally meet you.'

Liam was startled at first, but then decided he liked the look of what he saw and heard.

'Yes, Dylan, I can see now why you thought I had a photo of your mate here, instead of my cousin.'

''Old on, I ain't no relly of yours.'

'Sorry, of course you're not, you're Dylan's best mate and I hope we get to see a lot more of you in the future.'

'Grandy, please. Liam might not want to visit with us.'

Marie had been quietly watching as the three males sized each other up and now they were going to better each other to become king pin. She thought, *Yes John, you're still a boy at heart*, but she realised that that was probably what she loved about him the most.

At that point, the nurse walked in with the doctor close behind. 'Um, sorry to break up the party, but the doctor just wants to check Liam.'

John and Marie were heading for the door when Liam announced that they didn't have to leave. He was feeling fine, so the doctor wouldn't need much time, and he hadn't finished saying something to Dylan's grandfather. Marie smiled to herself as she thought, *Yes, something has worked. Liam has already started to loosen up.*

Chapter 25

'Good morning, Mrs Sims and congratulations on the birth of your beautiful twins.'

'Oh. Yes, thank you,' said Leila, nodding her head in the direction of Dr Hill who was now checking her medical charts at the end of the bed.

'Nurse, I'd like a close eye kept on the condition of Mrs Sims' wound, page me if you have any doubts.'

'Yes, doctor,' said the nurse as she finished redressing the wound.

'I'd also like her to have bed rest and restricted visitors for the next three days at least.'

'But, Doctor Hill, I'll be goin' home to the tribe today. I can't leave 'em with that nice young teacher for too long.'

With a slight movement of his head, as he reached for the nearest chair, Dr Hill dismissed the young nurse. His mind raced with thoughts of the conversation he was about to have with his patient. Before he even opened his mouth, Leila's expression was enough to have him wishing the floor would open up this very minute and swallow him whole.

'Mrs Sims, we ran into a bit of a problem after the birth of your twins. I'm afraid I didn't listen to you as intently as I should have during the past three or four months. Ah, well, you see, we had to remove a very large growth.'

Leila was quietly taking all this information in, but her eyes continually flashed confusion, so Dr Hill progressed as carefully as he knew how to.

'So, you see, Mrs Sims, after we'd taken what I hope was the extent of the growth, we found abnormalities with your ovaries as well. So to be cautious, we removed—'

'No. Nooo,' wailed Leila as she tried to get herself away from this situation, because in her mind, they had done something very, very, wicked to her body.

'Nurse, nurse,' Dr Hill called through the doorway to the nurse he had just asked to leave the room. 'I'll need someone to sit with Mrs Sims for a while. I've given her something to settle her down, but she'll still need watching carefully.'

'Yes, Doctor Hill. But why is she so upset?'

'Let's just say it's a mixture of native custom and religious belief that has been instilled into the young minds of many native people like Mrs Sims.'

'But, haven't you explained that what you did has probably extended her life, if not saved her life altogether?' asked the puzzled young nurse.

'I think time and logic will put the fear that Mrs Sims is experiencing at the moment to rest, hopefully forever.'

He then turned away from the nurses' station and headed in the direction of the nursery. In his mind, the pleasure of seeing the new babies far outweighed any hassle that was caused at the time they entered into the world. There was another male sitting beside the cribs that held the newest Sims children. He too found great pleasure in visiting the babies, but for a very different reason to that of Doctor Hill. The staff watched with fascination as he admired the babies. He had so much love for them and he was entranced so much that he failed to hear the Dr Hilll enter the ward.

'Ah, we meet at last!'

Liam's mind jolted back to reality as he turned to see who was interrupting his first visit with his new siblings.

'Sorry, mate. Did I startle you? I am the one who delivered these beautiful children.' He now offered his hand to Liam. 'They're doing really great.'

'Yeah. How's Mam? Why can't I go and see her yet?'

With this spark of tension, the babies became alarmed and both started howling in unison.

'Oh, boy! Think we'd both better make tracks before the staff come down on us like a ton of bricks.'

Both males made a very fast exit together, one being pushed and the other walking smartly behind.

'Your mum will be sleeping at the moment, but how about I take you there to her ward so you can see for yourself?'

Liam smiled as he realised that here was another adult that differed to the ones he usually met.

<h1 style="text-align:center">Chapter 26</h1>

Angie Dickson was mindlessly singing along with the radio that continuously played in her car as she changed lanes before turning into the neighbourhood streets where Di Brown had lived since her childhood. She always found this area had a friendly atmosphere, compared to the concrete jungle of inner city living, where she was currently staying with the Sims family. The people who lived here seemed to really take pride in and care for their environment. Lawns and gardens were neat and tidy, footpaths and gutters were clean and there didn't seem to be any resident graffiti artists about. The whole place had a calmness about it that brought out the best in all people, aged or young, sick or healthy. At this point, Angie's mind was racing in the world of if only and what if, but was quickly brought to a halt as she realised she'd just driven past Di's home. As Angie walked up the front path, something else made her realise just how different the lifestyle was for people living here: Di's front door was wide open. In Angie's neighbourhood this sight would enviably have a very sinister plot belonging to it: a robbery, a murder or even an early death that came uninvited into an over stressed life.

'Hello, Ang. How's life in the high-rise?'

'Oh, Di. Where do I begin to tell the sorry tale of the Sims family?'

But Di Brown had already anticipated how their lives would have affected the likes of Angie Dickson. So, talking was brought to a halt as she steered her guest through the house to a very pleasant outdoor room at the back of the dwelling.

'Gee, Di, I knew you had a green thumb, but this must have taken two green hands to cultivate.'

'Well, I have really! No, no, I've just kept things going since Donald passed away, but it's getting just a bit much to control, especially with full-time teaching. And no, I just couldn't give that up – well, not altogether.'

Now both women just sat admiring the garden in all its splendour. Two pair of eyes had become transfixed on the birdbath. A blackbird seemed to be schooling this season's young in the art of bathing, whilst also keeping an ever watchful eye for the local cat.

The spell was broken with Angie asking, 'Di, what do you use that building for? That one down on the left, it looks as though you have your own secret hideaway, for when times get tough.'

'How true that is! You see, Angie, Donald always thought that this place would become too much of a burden in our twilight years. So that was one of his last building projects: a completely self-contained, private two-bedroom unit with its own separate entrance. But as yet I haven't had the heart to look for suitable tenants that I would feel comfortable with living in the big house. You see, it doesn't suit most because it's too big for most families to contend with. My mum and dad, you see, had a large family. I was the youngest of eleven.'

'But you are still considering that, the house I mean, if you found someone suitable?'

Now the words were out and spoken aloud Angie's mind was exceeding the speed of light. She was too consumed with an idea that really had been there, well, forever, to see the puzzled look on her friend's face as she took the offered cool drink.

Chapter 27

'Sergeant Brothers, what are ya goin' to do with the truck? I mean, ya can't leave it here can ya?'

'No Sims, of course I can't. Do you have any idea what the cargo is, the stuff that's wrapped amongst the load of furniture back there?'

'Dunno, mate, I was only hitchin' a ride. Ya see, I'm 'tween jobs, ya might say.'

'Really, Sims! Now why doesn't that surprise me?"

'Look, mate, I really am just hitchin', otherwise do ya think I'd be stupid enough to wait around for ya all to turn up?'

'That's the thing that really has me puzzled.'

'What d'ya mean?'

'Sims, I think it's best if we don't discuss this matter until we get back to town. Let's wait till then. You can make an official statement in front of witnesses. Just in case some people get the impression that I might have pressured you or something like that.'

Ronnie thought better of giving a smart reply that was trying to force its way through his gritted teeth.

'Yeah, whatever. Do ya mind if I grab forty winks since I've got nothing to say and you're driving this thing wherever we might be heading?' he muttered as he clambered into the sleeping compartment, leaving the sergeant to drive in silence.

'Sergeant Brothers to base. Brothers to base. Over.'

Nothing returned but an eerie static sound until, 'One Tree here, Sarge. You must be outta range, can I help at all?'

'Thanks, One Tree, but no thanks. I've decided the best thing is to get this truck and passenger back to town. Thanks for your help before too. Over and out.'

Brothers couldn't help thinking how lonely life would be hauling these monsters back and forth across Australia, never knowing who or what you would meet along the way. Could this really be the reason that Sims was aboard, because he didn't fit the mould of interstate riders that he usually flagged down during traffic inspection check points?

'Sims. Hey, Sims. Wakey wakey, you going to hibernate back there forever? We'll be in town in about ten or fifteen minutes, thought maybe you'd like to freshen up a bit.'

'Um, yeah. Look, Brothers, what's goin' ta happen? Happen to me, I mean? Ain't a crime to hitch a ride out here, is it?'

'Let's just leave that 'til we get to the station. How about you just tell me a bit about you? I mean, you got family, or someone else you'd like to call?'

Brothers noticed at this point Sims definitely paled at the mention of family. Maybe, just maybe, he thought, this fella really was legit and was in the wrong place at the wrong time.

'Well, yeah! I mean, the missus may have had the kid by now. I mean kids, we're 'specting twins ya see.'

'Congrats, Sims. I'll see that you can make a phone call as soon as we get to the station. This can't be your first, or you would have been at the hospital?'

'Nah, not me mate. I wait till she brings 'em home. Can't

say I'm much good in them hospital places. They gives me the creeps.'

'Yeah, know what you mean. I have the same problem with dentists. Last year I passed out even before the treatment. The boys at the local have never let me live that one down. Don't suppose they ever will either.'

'Oh! I thought all youse coppers was real tough.'

Ronnie realised they were nearly to their destination when a few houses appeared together and now he could make out the local because of it having the biggest dish on the roof. Now as they rounded the corner there it was, the cop-shop with lock-up behind. A shiver ran the length of his backbone.

God, if you're still hearing me, help me get back to Leila, and I'll never do another dodgy thing, ever. I'll even go to mass with the tribe. I'll do anything, really I will.

Just as well Ronnie didn't know God doesn't do deals or he would never have had the courage to give the statement he was telling Brothers and that other pushy fella, who jumped on him every time Ronnie faltered or strayed from what he was telling them.

Chapter 28

Liam was overcome with relief as Dr Hill pushed him closer towards the sleeping figure attached to monitors and drainage tubes.

'Mam,' was all he managed before his pent up emotions overtook his small body. Leila stirred for an instant, but that was more than enough for Liam. Now, his furiously beating heart eased into calmness. His mum, his wonderful mother, would be alright. As they turned to leave the room, Liam was sure his mother smiled just for him.

'By the way, old man, how are you doing? It sure was a patch of bad luck that you ended up in hospital at the same time as the new kids made their entry into the world.'

'Yeah, s'pose. Hey, when can I go home?'

'Steady up, I'm not your doctor. But I can see you're itching to be gone from here. Tell you what, I'll check up with the doctor that you've been assigned to. Okay?'

'Yeah, sure. I mean yeah. That'd be great.'

'Hey, I didn't say you're going. But I will try.'

'It's just, well, I'm tired of all the questions. Ya see, I 'urt me arm a bit and me leg, but all of youse want to look at all of me. It's just not right, I mean, I got rights, don't I?'

'Easy on, Liam, don't get so upset. What do you mean, they want to look at all of you?'

'Well. It's Mrs Brown's fault, she had'ta see a couple of scratches on me back see, and now youse all wanna look.'

Doctor Hill quickly assessed what he'd been told and what he was hearing now. He thought it best to just go along with the conversation, to see where it was heading.

'Yeah, I know how you must be feeling. See this burn scar on my arm? Nothing much, is it? But let me tell you, it sure made history.'

'Really? But why?'

'Well, it happened way back, you know, when I was away at boarding school. Just because I wouldn't talk about it, or how it happened, everyone wanted to know all the details. And really, mate, it was none of their damn business.'

'That's it. That's just what they're doin' to me too. Makes me so mad.'

'Seeing that we've both been hassled, why don't we go to the kiosk and share a Coke or milkshake? My shout.'

Liam could not understand how different some adults were. He was even thinking that maybe they weren't all out to get kids like the usual ones he had contact with around his neighbourhood. Like the ol' ducks at the bingo, the fellas at the pool hall and especially the security guys at the shopping centre.

'Was that a yes, or are you dozing off?'

'Eh, watch it. I was makin' me mind up, and yeah, why don't cha. I'll have chocolate shake for me self though.'

'That's what I like, a bloke who knows his own mind and says what he thinks, and doesn't do it just 'cause everyone else is doing it.'

Dr Hill and Liam arrived at the kiosk and made their way to the counter to order.

'Hello, Doctor Hill,' greeted the bubbly young assistant, Cheryl. 'What will it be today?'

'One chocolate shake and, er … Oh why not, I'll have an iced coffee and two slices of that chocolate mud cake with a good heap of cream on the side. My new mate and I'll be sitting over there near the window, 'cause we've got serious men's business to discuss.'

Liam was suitably impressed with the order and was quite content to let the conversation drift in whatever direction the whim took it.

'Hey Doc, what 'appened to the kid? I mean, whoever did that to ya arm? Did the cops give ya a grill'n? How'd ya mates feel, I mean, after ya dobbed?'

Dr Hill paused to let the waitress deliver their order before replying, 'Ah, thanks Miss. Yes I think Liam and I can handle that amount of cream between us. What'd you think Liam?'

Doctor Hill waited patiently before saying any more to Liam, because, for some reason, Cheryl appeared to be hovering around their space. The tables she was so vigorously wiping down had had no patrons at all that day, as their surfaces actually glistened under the florescent lighting.

'Liam, did I say anything about dobbing? Now, did I really?'

'Well, no. But ya being smart and all, ya know, goin' to that fancy school and all.'

'Is that what you think, Liam? That I was having a great time at Clarkville College?'

'Geez, Doc. Don't go blow'n a fuse on me. I'm sorry, I jiz thought. I don't care about nuffin anyway.'

Their conversation came to a sudden halt, at the same time as a very loud noise was coming from the kitchen area. It sounded like a whole shelf of canned goods had abruptly collapsed, coupled with a deafening wail that quickly turned into peals of laughter. The two males were still eyeing each other when the young assistant raced back into the kiosk.

'Damned if I hadn't predicted that. You just wouldn't believe what happened.'

Doctor Hill found his voice as his eyes left Liam's face momentarily.

'What happened? Come on, tell us then before you start with that giggling fit again. That's something you'd never catch us men doing. Giggling, I mean.'

Luckily Cheryl didn't take offence, as she could see the admiration that had illuminated Liam's face as Doctor Hill spoke.

'Well. I've been telling the boss all week that we should be offering fruit salad as a special alternative sweet, because of an over-order. Well now, we'll have to because the temporary shelf just made its own decision.' Cheryl moved away, but her shoulders gave her away as they began shaking violently – yes, she was off again in another giggling fit.

'Umf, females. Stupid critters.'

'Yes, Liam, when I was your age that's about what I thought of girls, too. But let me warn you, mate, your attitude will change, just wait a few more years. You'll think differently.'

'Yeah maybe. Geez, this cake is good, Doc.'

Chapter 29

Angie sat absently twirling her drink, causing the ice cubes to rock back and forth in a rhythm that suited the peace and stillness that abounded in Di Brown's garden. A sudden explosion of splashing water and childish squeals of delight interrupted her thoughts. She swung around with such a force the remains of her drink and melting ice cubes were now seeping gracefully through the ground cover of native violets.

'I didn't know your neighbours had children.'

'Well, yes, they have,' Di replied cautiously, hoping she wasn't being overheard. 'They've had a really horrid time, waiting for officialdom to move.'

'Whatever do you mean, Di? Come on, come clean, you're not harbouring illegal spies next door are you?'

'It started when the parents fled their own country because of persecution. They had to leave their four children in the care of their grandmother. It was a case of hope for the best, you might say.'

'But didn't you tell me that couple had moved in nearly two and a half years ago with a baby born only late last year?'

'Yes, I did. Look Angie, I don't mean to seem rude, but do you mind if we take this conversation back inside the house? It's just I don't want them to overhear us talking about them and their problems.'

'Sorry, Di. Look, I wasn't trying to pry.'

'Of course not, Angie. In fact, I'm glad someone else knows now. It's felt like I've been carrying too many of other people's problems lately. You really are not prying, because I need to run some thoughts past you. Things that have really been causing me a lot of concern and heartache. Do you mind staying just a while longer? You could give the unit a phone call, just to let them know you haven't forgotten them.'

Angie was suddenly very aware that Di needed to confide in someone, but would she be able to offer any assistance to her dear friend? Di was certainly right about the house being of very large proportions, thought Angie, as she was now being ushered into the kitchen. *This kitchen table could easily seat twelve to fourteen people.* But then she thought, *It's probably still here because it would need to be dismantled to remove it from the house.* An audible sigh escaped from Di as she settled herself down on the chair next to Angie.

'Look, Di, if this is uncomfortable for you, I can forget I ever heard next doors' kids.'

'No, no, Angie. It's just, well … I feel sorry for those little kids. Who knows what they've had to go through? Maybe their persecutors will track them down. You see, as I'm the only neighbour, the authorities have seen fit to tell me just a brief outline of their circumstances. Forewarned is to be forearmed, is how they put it.'

'Warned! Di, what have you got yourself mixed up in now?'

'Nothing, nothing at all. Like I said, it's the kids who are the innocent players, and now they are destined to be lost in a mountain of red tape. They are not even allowed to venture past the fences, and there is a guard watching the house twenty-four hours a day. Imagine that, trapped in their own backyard.'

'That's horrible!'

Before Angie could regain control of her thoughts and more importantly her mouth, it was out. 'What you need here is a family of kids, so at least they could interact over the fence. Just so they know there is still a world going on.'

It was much too late now. The spoken thought was now out in the open, never to be restrained. Angie's hands flew to her mouth, but she couldn't hide the embarrassment that she could now feel creeping across her shoulders and up her neck with its tingly redness. Huge tears welled in her eyes, but when she focused on her friend she was sitting there just nodding and smiling.

'Oh, Di. Di, look, I'm so sorry, really I am. I should not have said any of that.' Angie was trying to escape from her friend's line of sight. At that very moment she felt lower than the belly of a snake.

'Thank you, Angie. Thank you, thank you.'

Her body wouldn't move as she was stunned into submission, as Di wrapped her arms around her shoulders. Now weeks, maybe months, of emotion was being unleashed as the older woman's body shook and shuddered. Angie stayed still, just returning the hug until the sobs were reduced to quiet crying. She knew she had said too much, but she'd never expected a reaction like this from Di. Wasn't she known at school as the rock for those who were floundering? She hoped with all her heart that their friendship had not been altered by her lack of thought when she'd aired the pipe dream that her mind had carried secretly for quite a while now.

Chapter 30

'Alright, Sims, I've been patient. I've listened to all this bull you've been spouting. Now I'm tired.' Sergeant Brothers leaned over the desk until Ronnie thought he was going to bite him. His fist slammed so hard and fast that it made the glasses of water vibrate with the rest of the desk. Ronnie sunk back further in the chair wishing it would swallow him whole.

'You're lucky it wasn't you I struck, Sims. How about you tell us the real story now, okay?'

'But,' he looked round at Sergeant Brothers hoping for a bit of moral support, 'I told ya, I was only hitchin'. Been told of a job up here, but like all me life, it turned out ta be a dud. What am I 'posed to have done anyway?'

'Not supposed, Sims!' yelled Bruce Evans, who had been quietly sitting in the room. 'Have done, did do and probably will do again. I'd be doing everyone a favour if I just put you in the cell out the back and, sort of, we might say, forgot I put you there. You know it's amazing, Sims, how quickly someone remembers what he ate last week when nature puts a bit of pressure on. Catch my drift, mate? I'm told it gets a might warm during the day but next to freezing in the dark. Brothers, weren't you telling me you thought the fan had packed it in, back in the cells, I mean? So, I'm sorry, Sims, you may be a little uncomfortable, we've got to attend a break-in, should be back in two or three days.'

Ronnie paled as the perspiration soaked his clothing. He was feeling very sick. But he held on to the only thing they couldn't take away from him: his confidence in himself.

'Lost your voice, Sims, or are you suddenly remembering what we'd like to know?'

'Hey, mate. How's a bloke 'posed to 'member what he don't know nuffin' about?'

'Oh you're good, Sims. We'll see what you can remember when we return. Jimmy will you take him out to the cells. Oh, and make sure there's nothing in the cell but our friend here, wearing only shorts and a t-shirt. That's right, nothing. No bedding, no shoes, no books, no nothing.'

'Ya can't do that. I've got rights.'

'Well, so you have, Sims. Jimmy, make sure he gets his regulation meals, but no visitors. Okay, Sims.'

The two officers left the room as Sims was left sitting there with his hands still handcuffed behind his back. In the back of his mind somewhere a voice spoke, *Keep to your story, Ronnie boy, keep to your story*. The side door now opened cautiously and Ronnie again paled at the sight coming though. Jimmy just happened to be two hundred and thirty centimetres of pure muscle. His dark arms glistened where they escaped the sleeves of his shirt. Ronnie couldn't help feeling like a mouse that just ran out of luck with the neighbourhood cat.

'Okay, Sims, this way.' Jimmy raised him up as though moving a fly. 'Stand still while I remove the cuffs, then you can take a shower in there and here's the clothes you'll wear. Just leave all your things on the floor. I'll bag them up later.'

'Hey. You can't really leave me in the cells, 'til you come back, I mean.'

'Sims, at the moment you don't have a whole lot of other options. Shower time's nearly up.'

'But I haven't even got in!'

'Smart boy, Sims. You're learning fast.'

Ronnie thought about complaining about the thing he was given for a towel, but a quick look at Jimmy changed his mind. As they walked to the back door of the police station, Ronnie suddenly realised the cell block was a completely separate building. He told himself, *Don't panic, cause they'd have ta have some sort of ventilation. It would be inhumane not to.*

Chapter 31

All the way home in the car, Marie felt as though she should pinch herself and then maybe she'd wake up in her favourite armchair, but it was John's voice that broke into her own private euphoria.

'Marie, you okay? You've not said a word since we left the hospital. Could you at least share your joke with Dylan and me because that grin has never moved? Come on, old girl.'

'Hey, not so much about old, remember we're the same age John.'

'Are you Nana? I always thought Grandy was the oldest!'

'Thank you, Dylan, dear.'

'Watch it, boy, crawlers don't last with me.'

John swung the car into the driveway, and then realised how pleasant it was living in the quiet street away from all the daily hustle and bustle of traffic and commuter's to-ing and fro-ing in their busy grind of life.

'Marie, dear, make us a cuppa while I put the car away.'

'Let me, Nana, let me.'

Without any further discussion, Dylan busied himself in the kitchen as Marie went into the bedroom to change into more comfortable shoes and revert back to her favourite cardigan.

'Well, Grandy, what did you think of Liam?' Dylan said as he was pouring the water into the teapot.

'Um ... Tell you the truth, I don't know boy.'

'John, don't be such a tease,' chipped in Marie as she came in to see John duck behind the newspaper to hide the smile plastered all over his face. But Dylan had stopped in an instant, thinking for a moment that his grandfather really meant what he just heard.

'Sorry, Dylan. But you're so easy to string along, not at all like your mate Liam.'

'What do you mean, Grandy?'

'Yes, John. Let's see you get out of this one.'

'Aw, don't be so critical, you two. What I meant was Liam does not trust people as openly as you, so he doesn't believe everything he hears, right? Liam would have seen straight away I was pulling your leg.'

Dylan sat down with his Milo and a look on his face as though suddenly he understood his friend just a bit better than he had before.

'Oh, I see!'

'The ward sister said that they'd like to keep Liam for a few extra days,' said Marie as she passed Dylan the plate of chocolate biscuits.

'Thanks, Nana. But Liam said he was feeling fine.'

'Yes I know, dear, but it seems there's a doctor there that thinks maybe he's close to finding out about who's been hurting Liam. So while his mum's still there, they can't see the harm in keeping him a few extra days. You're sure you don't know any more about this boy, Hill?'

'No, Nana, but I wish I did.'

'No, you don't, boy. It's not worth it to buy into someone else's trouble. Remember that.'

'John, did you think any more on that subject we were discussing before?'

Dylan flashed a look of puzzlement at his grandparents, but whatever it was they didn't seem to want to open the discussion before him. He noticed also that John just nodded and Marie smiled with satisfaction. It reminded him of the sort of secret code his parents used, but then it mostly meant a birthday surprise or unexpected cousins coming for a holiday.

'Hey, Grandy, what did you really think about Liam, I mean? He's great isn't he?'

'Well, Dylan, are you answering for me, or do you want to know what I thought?'

A shocked look travelled across his face before he realised that Grandy was just fooling again, so he tried Nana's trick and tried to ignore the feeling welling up inside him.

'Marie, look, look what you've done. You've brainwashed my grandson into reacting just like you.' John turned again to face Dylan. 'I think he's a fine friend for you to have. I bet he'd never leave his friends when they needed help. In fact, if I'd wanted to hand-pick a best mate, I couldn't have done better myself.'

A quick look in Nana's direction reassured Dylan that his grandfather was not trying to pull his leg this time.

'And yes, Marie, the answer is yes, but not straight away. Maybe in a few weeks, okay?'

Again, Dylan saw the secret looks that were being passed between his grandparents. How he wished he could break into the code all adults seemed to use when they communicated above the understanding of children.

'Bet I could make a fortune,' he muttered to himself not realising he'd said it out loud.

'What was that, old man?'

'Nothing, Grandy. Think I'll go and read my book as my back feels as though it needs some down time for a while.'

Chapter 32

The second Angie entered the corridor on the tenth floor, she knew something was not quite right. There was no deafening volume of rap music, no crying of unhappy youngsters. As she drew nearer, the door at the entrance to Mr Black's unit was, unusually, wide open.

"Scuse me Miss, could you spare a moment? You're the one called Angie, ain't ya?'

Stumbling with shock or rather embarrassment, she turned around quickly.

'Yes. You're Mr Black, I assume? There's nothing wrong with the kids is there?'

'Far from it, Miss. It's a bloomin' miracle what you've done.'

'Sorry, Mr Black, I'm not following. What are you talking about?'

'The welfare miss, they was 'ere.'

Now panic was racing through Angie. She was blaming herself for staying away longer than she expected.

'Mr Black what did the kids get up to? Remember they're only kids. Surely it couldn't have been bad enough for you to call the welfare department. Have you no heart, Mr Black?'

'No miss, you've got it all wrong. I didn't. They had another family to see on the eighth floor, so they just called to see how you were managing. See, they know what a 'andful them can be.'

'But … Where are they? Where are my friends, the two women who were helping me with the kids?'

It was Mr Black's turn to look totally embarrassed and he couldn't bear to look Angie in the face.

'Mr Black, please, just tell me what happened.'

'Well, miss, it wasn't like I was snooping or anything, but I did 'ear 'em say something about a phone call from some place I never 'eard of, something to do with the police.'

'Oh, not now. Not now everything is finally working out for the family. Mr Sims wasn't hurt, was he?'

'Dunno, miss. They just gathered the kids and your friends together and left.'

'But, Mr Black … You must know where they've gone.'

Suddenly, Angie realised how old and frail the man appeared and here she was badgering the daylights out of him in his own home.

'Look, I'm real sorry Mr Black, but you sort of shocked me. Now I'm worried about what has happened. Maybe my friends left a note for me. Oh. Here, Mr Black, take this. If they come back or you hear anything before I do, please give me a phone call. Thanks again.'

Then she hurried past the puzzled man, intent on trying to figure out what on earth had happened in the last forty-five minutes since she'd left Di's house and came straight back here. It was a strange feeling turning the key and not hearing the kids she had grown to love in the short time she had been with them. Angie opened the door expecting the place to be in a shambles because of the hurried departure, but no, everything was very tidy. Something just wasn't making any sense to her at all. But wait, maybe there was an answer. Sitting propped up next to the coffee jar on the kitchen bench was an envelope with her name on it. She quickly started to tear it open as her hands trembled with the fear of unknown dread.

Dear Angie.

Don't be alarmed, there's nothing wrong with the kids. We're going with them. The Department has been advised that Mr Sims is being held at a police station somewhere in the Northern Territory. He's 'helping' with some sort of enquiries. You know how hard it is to stop the department wheels once they have been put in motion.

Give us a ring as soon as you can.

Angie felt as though she had just hit a brick wall head on at full speed. In fact, she had to pick up the note and read it again, and still it didn't penetrate her brain. Nothing was making any sense at all. What had Mr Sims done and why was he in the Northern Territory? Had anyone been to inform Mrs Sims yet? She hoped not, because then Liam would also know and it didn't bear thinking about how he would react to all this news. Her head had begun to spin and tears were running down her face unnoticed until one dropped on to the paper causing the words to blur inside the damp blob. *This is not good*, she chastised herself, *crying won't help anyone at this moment. Now pull yourself together Angie, you need to be strong. The kids need you now more than before. Drat, where'd I put that mobile?*

Chapter 33

'Ya know what, Doc, that cake was nearly as good as the ones my mam makes every week.'

'Really, Liam? Tell me, how does she ever find the time, with all you kids to see to?'

'Wha'd ya mean? Dylan ain't been yapping to ya, 'as he?'

For a moment, Doctor Hill was losing the thread of this conversation. *Better make a move,* he was thinking.

'Liam, how do you feel if we go and sit outside and talk? I just can't think straight with all that hilarity going on in the kitchen.'

'Uh … yeah okay, it's fine with me, doc.'

Thank goodness I escaped that sticky situation, he thought as he pushed Liam through the door and round the corner.

'How about here? We can watch those pesky ducks down near the river while we solve the woes of the world.'

'Sure, Doc.' Liam was a little edgy about talking.

'Now, where'd we get to? Oh yeah, you thought I was a dobber.'

'Nah, not really. But tell me again, think I missed a bit.'

'Well, you see, I was the smallest in my class, so naturally I copped a bit when no one was looking. But then this new kid came. I didn't like him at all.'

'Why, Doc? Was he a spaz?'

'Liam. I will pretend I didn't hear that. I found maths and science classes a whole lot of fun – you know, all of a sudden things made sense to me. Well, after our term tests, the other kids found this new kid wasn't as smart as he told them he was, and when he found out I did okay in the tests, he said he'd really like to be my best mate.'

'So, ya had a best mate? I've got heaps of 'em.'

'Do you want to know what happened or not Liam?'

'Geez, not if you're gunna get mad at me.'

'You know what, Liam, I think I'm wasting my time.'

Doctor Hill was now standing up preparing to go and leave Liam to his own frustrations.

'Hey, Doc, bet that fella didn't cause you as much hassle as Hilly does to me.'

Oh my God, thought Doctor Hill, *what do I do now?*

'Please, Doc, I really wanna tell someone,' whispered Liam, with a very distinct waver in his voice.

'It's okay, mate, I'm ready to listen if you're ready to talk,' he said as he moved Liam's wheelchair as far away from the main thoroughfare of people moving between the hospital buildings.

'First off, Doc, I need ta know ya won't go runnin' off yellin' to the cops or nuffin'.'

'Why, Liam? Do you think I might need to?'

'Nah. Jis don't want me mates ta think I dobbed. Cause I can take care of me self, always have 'til I met up with Hilly.'

'Okay, tell me how you met him, that wouldn't be dobbing and I'd really like to know how and where you met this Hill boy.'

Liam was feeling really uncomfortable, but he knew in his heart that if he didn't trust this man with his story it would keep him captive forever.

'Well, one night I'd just had enough of the babies' noise. See, I was s'posed to finish this project for Mrs Brown— that's me teacher—and Suzy went and knocked her bowl of icecream and topping all over me work and I'd jis finished it too. Well, I jis did me nut 'cause it made me mad, so I jis ran out and ran and ran.'

Doctor Hill sat and listened to all this frustration that was pouring out of this young man.

'And I ended up down behind the football clubrooms. It seemed quiet, ya know, nobody about and all, so I sat down next to the dump bins and the back door. Next thing I hear this kid getting done over. It was a real bad fight. I couldn't jis sit there, could I? I mean, if I was copping it I'd like someone to help out.'

'But, Liam—'

'Ya said ya'd jis listen.'

Doctor Hill nodded in silence, wishing he knew how he was going to handle this unwanted knowledge.

'Well, it was Hilly wasn't it! He was givin' this other kid a real thumping, so I yelled at him. With the distraction the other kid took off, then Hilly came over to where I was. After he mouthed off at me he seemed to realise I weren't taken no notice. That's when the trouble started. He asked if I wanted to earn a bit on the side. Course I said yes, didn't I, before I even asked what I had to do. When he finished explainin' it sounded dead easy. It's then I shoulda 'membered what me dad always says about easy money, but I didn't. All I could think of was the dollars. Ya see, all I had ta do was deliver these big envelopes and sometimes a small box and wait for somefing to bring back to Hilly.'

'But, Liam, didn't you ever wonder or at least think about what it was you were delivering? Surely you didn't think you were just playing a game of postman!'

'Well, no ... It was easy and money was great.'

'Why does Hilly want to hurt you now?'

'Umm … A few months back, he gives me a couple of extra deliveries and I brought back the envelope like usual, but this other fella was there instead of Hilly. Said he'd taken over. Next day, Hilly turned up with a split lip, and that's when he started makin his threats an usin' his knife and lighter.'

Liam was now totally exhausted, but it did feel better now that he had finally told some of his story. Doctor Hill didn't say a word, but just pushed Liam back to his ward and then left. He made a note in his diary to go and have a chat to that nurse who worked on the kid's ward, because he remembered hearing how her son had been in the police force before going to the Middle East.

Chapter 34

'Hi Mum, it's Bruce ... No, I'm fine. In fact, I'm back in Australia, so we'll be able to catch up a bit, but not straight away. No, Mum, I'm not in any strife ... There is something you could do for me. In fact, it would be a really, really big help. See, I met this fella who said his wife was expecting twins. I know it's a long shot, could you check at the hospital for me. The name he told me was Sims ... Really? You know, she's a patient and her son, too. Maybe you could tell me what you know about them, you know, general background stuff ... Thanks, Mum, I'll ring you back in a couple of hours, okay.'

Jill Evans was so surprised to hear from her son, especially as she thought he was still in the Middle East, and how could he know Mrs Sims' husband? With all these questions whirling in her brain she realised that she'd let Bruce hang up without getting a contact number. Jill was considering what the best plan of action was when it was taken out of her hands. First, it was the staff from the roster room, begging that she delay the time of her holiday for a few days. Second, Doctor Hill tapped and entered her office.

'Oh, am I glad I've caught you before you left.'

'Doctor Hill, what can I possibly do for you? I can assure you there are no patients requiring your services here.'

He looked blankly at her before the smile crept across his face and then they were both laughing. It hadn't occurred that being a specialist in gynaecology would cause such mirth in the children's ward.

'I'm sorry, it was you personally I wanted. No, ah … I mean your knowledge of one of your patients.'

'Look, I was just about to go and grab a bite to eat now that my holiday plans have now been put on hold.'

As they were walking out the door, Doctor Hill turned to Jill and smiled as he asked that things be kept very informal, starting with first names only. He thought, *Did I just witness the slightest colour of a blush ascend from her throat to her cheeks?*

'Yes, Doctor … um .. Paul. But, I really can't think how I will be of any help to you.'

Jill became even more puzzled when he guided her past the cafeteria and headed towards one of the doctors lounges. He then satisfied her curiosity by adding, 'It will be more private here. It's one of the patients on your ward that I want to speak about. Liam. Liam Sims, to be precise.'

At this point, Jill felt herself relax as well as wonder how Doctor Hill had become involved. Then it struck her like a bolt of lightning. Of course, he was Leila's doctor.

'You've seen the scarring on his back, no doubt.'

Jill sat nodding her head as Paul continued.

'For some reason, unknown to me, he has chosen to trust me. That poor little kid has been to hell and back, so much so that I'd say he was dash lucky that he had that accident at school.'

'I still don't see how I can be of any assistance, Doc—Paul.'

'Oh, but you can. One of your sons is in the police force, isn't he?'

'No. Actually, he's joined a religious group, and until I got a phone call this morning, I thought he was still in the Middle East.'

'Can I be really rude and ask what he wanted and would I be able to speak to him? Please, it is important.'

Jill didn't answer straight away and Paul could see the confusion that clouded her face. To give her some time and space, he walked across the room to make a couple of coffees and grabbed a couple of packs of sandwiches from the well-stocked fridge of the doctors lounge. Sitting down, he offered them to Jill and broke the ice by asking if she needed sugar for her coffee.

'Look, Paul, I don't know what's going on. First you save the life of Mrs Sims, then you become the confidant of Liam who won't talk to anyone else about his injuries, then my son, Bruce, phones me out of the blue asking for my help with your patient, Mrs Sims, and tells me he's met someone called Sims. Now I can't get in touch because I was so shocked I forgot to ask where he was. I don't even know why he has returned from his missionary work.'

Neither of them had realised how long they'd been sitting there, thrashing and sifting their problem about, until Paul's pager screeched with its shrill voice. Quick apologies were exchanged from both sides, during which Paul wrote down his mobile number together with his pager number. It was his insistence that he needed to talk to her son that put the deep worry lines across her face, and she noticed for the first time how much of a headache she had. Kids, even when they've left home, still cause worry and anxiety.

<h1 style="text-align:center">Chapter 35</h1>

Angie read the note again: *Northern Territory, jail, helping, give us a ring*. Were all the Sims family magnetised for trouble? With this she wondered if her pipe dream would ever become a reality. *Stop it, Angie, stop at once,* she chastised herself. Now think, what line should she follow first? Of course, ring Barbara and Helen, but would they be at the women's shelter or somewhere else? *Blast the budget this week*, she thought, *I'll ring their mobile. I'll just have to keep it to a short call.* Angie picked up the mobile phone and dialled Helen's number.

'Hello, Helen, yes, it's Angie. What the hell has been going on? Are the kids alright? What's happened to Mr Sims? What are the police doing?'

'Angie, have you got a pencil? Now write this number down, get off your mobile phone and relax, take a couple of deep breaths and call me back on the Sims' landline.' Angie was using her mobile, and she didn't like wasting time on it because of the cost involved.

'Hello, Angie. Gee, I'm glad you got rid of motor mouth.'

'Yeah. Well, I was worried and you know how strict my budget is now that I've finished the relief teaching.'

'Now, what question would you like answered first?'

'Oh, Helen! I'm really sorry, but it really threw me for a sixer, especially when Mr Black was being really nice, even concerned for the kids.'

'Well, the welfare was informed by the Territory police that Mr Sims was with them, helping solve a crime. They knew Mrs Sims wasn't home and they had to have a piece of the confusion.'

'Where are the kids now? What's happening?'

'The kids are having a ball. Suzy even got to say hello to her dad via police radio room, while the others were checking out the police car, siren, lights, and the works.'

'But it makes me sound redundant.'

Helen was quick to pick up the ever so slight quiver in Angie's voice, but chose not to be drawn into her friends anguish at that moment.

'It's a shame you're feeling like that Angie. Barbara and I could do with about an hour to ourselves because we're stuffed. If you could see the room at the police station, you'd also understand that we have outworn our welcome a million times already.'

'Look, Helen, why did you let me prattle on so much. I'm totally embarrassed now. Are the kids allowed to come back to the unit? What's Mr Sims doing in the Northern Territory at a police station, no less?'

'The sergeant here has told the kids if they were really good he'd bring them back home in the prisoner transport vehicle. Since then, I've not heard a peep. The officer who will come with them will probably be able to answer all the questions. Oh, and Angie, spruce up a bit 'cause he's real spunky.'

'Get off, Helen. You'll keep.' As she hung up she found herself smiling.

Chapter 36

John and Marie got down to some really serious discussing about what would be the best way to handle the plan they were cooking.

'Are you really sure, Marie?'

'I think you're the one having reservations, but then that's how you always sift through every little detail and that's what I love about you.'

'Love you too, but right now I need to look over some of my papers.'

'John. Couldn't you put the family history tree on hold for a few weeks?' All she saw was John's back as he headed out to his beloved papers.

Marie busied herself washing up and thinking about what she would prepare for the evening meal. In the quietness her mind began to work overtime and none of it involved food. She went down the hall to check on Dylan and as she suspected his eyes had failed and sleep had won. Marie carefully placed a rug over Dylan. He sighed once and settled back to a comfortable position. It was at times like this she thought about Liam. Did anyone hold and comfort him? But then she thought, *No, Liam couldn't, in his mind he had to be tough. I do hope this scheme we're working on will turn out for the best, and not backfire and cause more harm.* Flicking on the radio, Marie was about to change to her favourite CD that always had a calming influence, but something the announcer said brought Marie to a complete standstill. Of course, she should have made more of an effort to become a friend of Leila. Marie had no idea how tough it must be trying to keep a family together when according to Di Brown Leila's family had wiped their hands of her when Liam's birth was evident.

John was calling out excitedly. 'Marie. Marie. Where are you, woman?'

'John, keep your voice down. Dylan's resting and calm down before your blood pressure goes through the roof.'

'Sorry. Marie, I want you to think back to your childhood.'

'Really, John? You know I don't have the same interest as you in old family skeletons.'

'What about school holidays that you spent at Marsh Flats?'

'Um … No, I can't recall just now. Why is it important that I remember now?'

'No, Marie. I don't want to prompt you. I need it to be your own memory, just to confirm what I think I've found.'

'Out, John. Out of my kitchen. This is my domain and I won't be bullied.'

'Okay, but please think on what I've asked. Marsh Flats.'

Marie's temper that had begun to simmer was now fast reaching boiling point. She loved John but sometimes he could be infuriating. Calling from the doorway, Marie told John she needed to go for a walk to clear her head. The happy sounds of children playing in the playground zapped Marie back to the present, but with it she was becoming aware of memories swirling through the mist of a long lifetime. Yes, that whistle, she knew that whistle. Looking at the children she was shocked to see it was the small girl standing on top of the monkey bars that was emitting that piercing sound. Marie remembered staying with her aunt and uncle at Marsh Flats and the fun she had had with her cousins, Anne, Beth and their older brother Ronald.

Chapter 37

Ronnie was sweltering in his confined space. As Jimmy watched on the video surveillance camera, he was convinced Ronnie's condition was seventy per cent worry and anxiety, and thirty per cent climate conditions. He remembered what Sergeant Brothers and that new fella had said: 'No contact with the detainee for a least six hours.' It didn't make any sense at all to Jimmy – if the bloke's guilty, he's guilty, full stop. Maybe after growing up in the conditions he saw most of his relatives live in, no one would blame his thinking. It was hard and confusing for Jimmy. He didn't belong with his mother's people, but then he didn't with his father's people either. It was pure chance that his father had been given an opportunity for work, thus taking them away from the small community that never let Jimmy forget he didn't belong. Leaving the air-conditioned part of the police station always made him appreciate the hardship his mother's people lived with every day. It also reflected how his father had taught Jimmy to cherish the value of his self-worth.

Ronnie jumped as Jimmy threw open the viewing slot in the steel door. The two men eyed each other; both could see the terror contained within but for different reasons.

Ronnie could contain his silence no longer. 'Brothers? Where's Brothers an' that other fella?'

Jimmy just stood, showing no emotion whatsoever, although his personal terror was eating him alive.

'Com' on!' Ronnie shouted.

Jimmy raised his hand and started to close the slot. Terror consumed Ronnie as he buckled to the ground, 'I'll 'elp Brothers, I'll talk to 'im.'

Ronnie was now crying and sobbing as Jimmy had never seen a man, other than his father when he and Jimmy returned home to find what a gang of hooligans had done to their home, before turning their hatred onto his mother. It almost broke his father's spirit, but it instilled a goal in life for Jimmy, as they buried his mother.

'Hey, mate. Take it easy. Brothers' just radioed to say they'd be back within two hours. I thought you might like to come and have a shower and share a meal with me.'

Ronnie couldn't believe it. Was there really a God? Was He really giving him a second chance? Jimmy now opened the cell door to find Ronnie was on the floor, sitting on his heels, holding his head and rocking his body back and forth. Jimmy could sense this man had reached a turning point in his life, but he hoped his spirit had not been broken. In a voice that didn't sound like his own, Ronnie asked what was on the menu.

'What's your choice, barra or buffalo?'

'Either. But I think I would have killed you on the spot if you had offered pizza.'

Jimmy could not reason with this comment, but tucked it away in his brain, as intuition said it was important.

Ronnie couldn't believe how much he was enjoying the shower until Jimmy's voice boomed over the sound of the water.

'Food's up. You'll be looking like a prune soon.'

Both men were still sitting in Jimmy's office, having just finished their meal of barramundi when Sergeant Brothers returned.

'Do you feel like having our little chat now, Sims?'

'How do I know my kids and Leila won't be hurt if I do?'

'But if you were only hitching a ride, who would want to do anything like that?'

'Stop playing games, Sims. We're wasting time and the trail is getting cold,' Bruce Evans said as he loomed over Ronnie.

'Okay. Yeah, I thought there was something fishy, but honest I never, never saw any of the merchandise.'

Evans was taking over the questioning now. 'Look, Sims. At the moment you're our only contact with the traders.'

'But … I really don't know …'

'Shut up and listen, Sims.' Evans was getting worked up. 'Where was the driver going to take his load? What did the driver and the pilot argue about? Who arranged this little drive for you?'

'I was never told the plans, just told where to be.'

'How did you get caught up in this market? Because you just don't seem the right type.'

'It was sorta by accident. I was sitting on the steps outside the unit.'

'My sources gave me a name, but so far we've been unable to track him down and make anything stick. The name I've been given is Angelo.'

When the name had been spoken out loud Ronnie thought he'd come to the end of his time on this earth. All three investigators noticed the quick change in Ronnie Sims.

'Hey, Ronnie, is that why you said you'd kill me if I offered pizza?' quizzed Jimmy.

'So, you do know our friend. Do you realise how many young lives he and his cronies ruin?'

Evans was still very confused and worried.

'Before I say anymore, I want to know my family will be taken care of. You don't understand how much I love Leila and the kids.' Tears were streaming from Ronnie's eyes.

Jimmy made the suggestion that they take a coffee break for ten minutes or so.

Chapter 38

Angie thought about what Helen and Barbara had said, about how the department had stuck their nose in without being asked. It gave her just that touch more courage to speak again to Di.

'Hello, Di, yes, it's Angie. I'd like to run something past you, but please stop me if I'm exhausting our friendship.'

'Of course, Angie, but I don't think you could possibly do that.'

Di Brown sat back in her favourite chair as she listened to the plans that had been gathering forces in not only Angie's head, but her own as well. When Angie had finished talking, there was silence for a few moments.

'Have you finished, Angie?'

'Oh … I shouldn't have pushed so hard. I'm sorry.'

'But, Angie, I'm surprised how accurately you've been reading my mind. I'll make sure I don't think too much when I'm around you next.'

'Wha-what do you mean? I mean—what are you saying Di?'

'I would love to be able to help give the Sims family a chance that they seemed to have always missed out on.'

'Are you saying what I think you're saying, Di?'

'That depends. If you think I'm going to leave this huge family home locked up and empty, you're wrong. You see, I've already moved myself into the unit you saw at the end of the garden the last time you called round.'

'Are you sure? I mean … I didn't, or I hope I didn't, put unnecessary pressure on you. You know how I always speak my mind and then wish I hadn't.'

'Angie, I wish the world was full of a lot more people like you. When I went to the hospital to visit Liam and his mum, it took a lot of willpower not to blurt out the plans that were hatching in my head ever since you described their living conditions.'

'Di, are you really sure? I mean, there will probably be quite a lot of red tape to cut through, especially as the welfare knows my two friends and I have been looking after them recently. Helen and Barbara are bringing the kids home shortly, would you believe, in a police prisoner transport vehicle! Perhaps I could mention what we plan to do to the officer when he comes.'

'If you think it will help, Angie.'

Angie felt she needed to change the subject for a while. 'Di, how are your neighbours doing?'

'They were what tipped my thinking about the Sims.'

'Sorry, I'll have to go. I can hear Suzy and the others at the door. Bye, talk to you soon Di.'

The kids poured in, creating their usual chaos and noise.

'Hello, you must be the infamous Angie,' the officer said as he offered his hand to her. 'Officer Tim Cook, at your service.'

Was he mocking her with the low bow and sweeping arm movement?

'Could I please have a few quiet moments with you? Although I don't know if you can help.'

Officer Cook was immediately put on the defence, not knowing what to expect.

'A mutual friend who has a rather large home is willing to allow the Sims family to rent instead of these cramped conditions in these cement boxes. Would there be any problems with the welfare department?'

'When would these new arrangements take place, do you think?'

'I hadn't thought. I mean, the department could say no, couldn't they? As the kids are still under their jurisdiction.'

'Look, the kids seem to have settled down now. How about you let me take this back and run it past some of my superiors?' Officer Cook asked, as he could hardly believe his luck at hearing this information. 'Oh, by the way Angie, this mutual friend would still have to have a police check. You know, protect the kids!'

Angie smiled as she told him, 'That would be no problem at all.'

Chapter 39

B ruce Evans declined the offer of coffee and left the room momentarily as he thought, *Must give Mum another ring. She may be able to shed some more light on this man, Sims.*

Meanwhile Jimmy, Sergeant Brothers and Ronnie were enjoying each other's company, rather like good mates than, in reality, hunters versus hunted.

'I say Jimmy, did you let Ronnie make his phone call?'

'Oh. Sorry, Boss, can't say that I did.'

'No matter. You can have your call now if you like.'

Now Ronnie's mind was swirling. *Do I ring the unit, hospital or maybe Angelo, to give him a warning?* He decided on the unit because whoever was there would be able to answer all his questions, even if it meant listening above the chaos of his kids that Leila called the tribe. Ronnie was still puzzling over who might be in the unit and what he would say to this stranger. Evans rejoined the three other men, unsure of the reaction he may get. At the same time, Ronnie had replaced the phone for the third time. Now Ronnie was really worried, remembering the threatening stare and menacing words Angelo had spat out. Surely he wouldn't hurt his kids; they were completely innocent. Ronnie could see now how deeply he had become involved with Angelo's dark world of crime. He had become addicted to the extra money that the taxman didn't know about. So much so that he'd blocked the reasoning, conscious voice inside his head. Evans didn't have to wait long for the anticipated reaction, as he walked across the room, Ronnie started shouting, 'The devils have got me kids. Me life is worth nothing now. How will I ever face Leila knowing it was me utter stupidity that has taken them from us?'

The three others in the room were taken aback by this avalanche of anger. Evans withheld the information he'd just received, hoping this distraught man may divulge more of what he knew or didn't know.

'Sims. What do you mean? The devils have got your kids! How do you know this?'

Jimmy was the first to notice that Ronnie's spirit was breaking. He had to do something to help, so he asked Ronnie, 'Sims, think back to when you last saw the pilot and the truck driver, did they exchange anything?'

'Ah … Yeah … I think so,' Ronnie replied, trying to recall the event.

At this, Bruce Evans swung round. 'Jimmy, what were you thinking?'

'I was thinking that maybe the pilot was injured as well.' Jimmy answered.

'Perhaps we should see if the driver is in a state of talking yet. It may be all we will ever get,' said Bruce.

'Hey, you lot! What about me kids?' shouted Ronnie in a wild panic.

The offer was put to him. If he helped break the chain of these smugglers, the court may be lenient on him, perhaps even dismiss him altogether as an innocent hitchhiker in the wrong place at the wrong time. Sergeant Brothers and Jimmy left Evans with Ronnie.

'Hey, Sarge. Is it alright to leave them alone? I mean, Ronnie looks as though he has learnt it tough on the streets.'

'S'pose we'll just have to trust Evans.'

Jimmy had a bad feeling about leaving Ronnie, and asked Sergeant Brothers if he could return earlier to fix up a few papers.

Chapter 40

Marie stood with her hands resting on the cold, galvanised fence, transfixed with the antics of the group of children playing in the playground.

"Ey, what ya lookin' at, lady?'

This startled Marie, because she hadn't realised one of the children was now standing beside her. Marie tried to explain that she wasn't really watching, but more like dreaming of her grandson and if he would soon be able to do the same playing.

'Is he a baby?'

'No. He was badly injured on his family's cattle station.'

'Oh … Well, I s'pose it's okay to watch.'

After watching a little longer, Marie continued to walk, trying to think of whatever John wanted her to remember about school holidays spent at Marsh Flats. Marie was now feeling a little drained of energy, so she was glad to find a vacant bench near the fountain. The pigeons began cooing and strutting around her feet. *Oh, you poor things.* She wished she had a few crumbs for them.

Feeding the chooks and gathering the eggs, and then finding a broody hen that I claimed to be mine while I patiently waited for the eggs to hatch, Marie thought, *Surely that is not relevant to John's tree.* Then a few more moments of childhood began appearing within her head. She and Beth had continued their friendship 'til just a few years ago, when a sudden illness took her away from this earth. Anne changed in her late teens; she was supposed to be bridesmaid at Marie and John's wedding, but declined suddenly. Since their brother Ronald died in the fire, Anne had become very secretive, often disappearing for days on end, and just returning as though nothing different had happened. Beth and her parents were shocked and puzzled when out of the blue she announced she knew of a young man she would like to give Ronald's clothes to. Not all of them, just enough, because he had nothing. Her Dad had asked her to bring this young fellow home; he might have been able to offer a bit of work. Now Anne became very defensive and demanded they just trust her as there was no way this man would come to the house. He still had his pride, but nothing else. The family had found it very strange when they began tying up the things that had belonged to Ronald. His bank account had been closed ten days before the fire. Anne was the registered owner of his vehicle. When questions became more difficult for Anne to evade, she packed up and told her parents she'd been offered a job that was too good to turn down. No forwarding address was given as she said, 'I'll let you know when I'm settled.' Then the grieving parents felt they had lost their only son and perhaps one of their daughters as well. They supposed it was harder for Anne because she and Ronald had been best mates with each other.

Chapter 41

As the nurse helped Liam back into bed, she noticed that he seemed completely exhausted.

'Liam, you sure you feel alright?'

'Yeah, but me arm is 'urting.'

'I can fix that for you, but you seem to be so unhappy.'

'S'pose. I 'avent seen Dilly. Maybe he's got a new friend now.'

'But I thought that was the boy you said was causing all that abuse to you.'

'No, *Dilly*. Not Hilly. Me friend, Dylan.'

'Oh! The boy that came in with his grandparents. Liam, how about you just lay back and have a rest, and I'll check if I'll be able to take you to visit with your mum and the babies.'

'Yeah, great, I'd luv to.'

Now the nurse was called to another patient. Liam turned 'til he was in a comfortable position, and sighed once before sleep overtook him quickly. His was not a restful sleep, because it was in his sleep state that the most terrible nightmares claimed his mind. In reality, Hilly was about the same size as Liam, but when Liam slept, he turned into a monster that could shoot fire bursts from his fingertips. His thumbnails became knife blades. With these thoughts tearing through him, Liam didn't sleep too long. When the nurse realised he was awake again, she came to take him to the maternity ward. Liam exploded when she suggested he have a bit of a wash and change his pyjamas.

'Liam, it was only a suggestion. I don't mind if you want to see your mum when you're all sticky and with smelly clothes.'

'I'll only change if I do it me self.'

'I wasn't even offering, Liam. So, I guess the laugh is on you.'

'Wha' ya mean? I'm not laughing.'

'No, Liam, but I am because I can see the look on your face.'

'Nick off.'

'Oh, Liam. I didn't mean to upset you, but you see, I had forgotten about the unmentionable back!'

The nurse then bent down and got some new pyjamas from the bottom drawer before she went away to get a dish of warm water and a couple of towels.

After Liam had finished, the nurse came back to remove the soapy water and put the towels and clothes in the laundry container. As she helped him into the wheelchair, she spoke quietly near his ear.

Chapter 42

Helen and Barbara couldn't wait to be alone with Angie, but Officer Cook seemed to have a never-ending stream of questions.

'Well, thank you again, Angie. I'll be in touch,' he said as he finally left and closed the door.

The kids were joining in creating a terrible din. Angie put her hands over her ears and literally had to shout at the top of her voice to regain some sort of control.

'Okay, troops. I think its enemy inspection time. Suzy, I'm putting you in control while I have a chat with Helen and Barbara.'

The three women left the children in the lounge room area while they went to the kitchen. Helen put the kettle on while Barbara got out the mugs and also produced two Boston buns she'd thought to purchase on their way to the unit. They couldn't contain their curiosity anymore and instantaneously they both uttered the same thought.

'That officer Tim Cook is spunky, isn't he?'

'I thought it was very nice of him to bring you and the

children home,' replied Angie. As all her life she had been very wary of showing emotion too quickly, she could think of many times when she'd been hurt rather badly.

'Aw ... Come on, Ang,' rushed far too quickly past Helen's lips. Because she saw the hurt in her friend's eyes but also embarrassment colouring her face, Helen changed the subject by asking if she needed to spread the slices of bun for the children.

'No. No they'll just eat the bun as it is.'

'Angie,' Barbara said, 'what did Officer Cook mean when he said "Can our mutual friend pass a police check"?'

'Can't say just yet, but it could be a heaven-sent blessing for some people.'

'Now who's being secretive?' Helen piped in.

'No, please don't ask questions. You'll both be the first to know if and when it happens.'

Bang, bang, bang on the door sent Suzy rushing towards the women in the kitchen. The others all headed for the bedrooms. Angie went to the door wondering who could possibly be there. Surely the welfare weren't hounding them again already.

'Why, hello, Mr Black,' Angie said upon opening the door.

'Hello, Miss, I just had to come and see if the little tykes were alright. Gee, Miss, you've worked miracles on the unit as well as the young'ns.'

'Well thank you, Mr Black. Come in, we're just having a cuppa.'

At that moment, Suzy raced from the kitchen to find the others in the bedrooms.

'Mr Black's here. Blackie's inside. Angie asked him to have a coffee and he said yes.'

'Suzy, can we go and see him? If Angie has let him in, it must be okay.' The children crept out of the bedroom and towards the newly arrived Mr Black, curious to see why Angie had invited him in.

'Well well, this is the first time I've seen them all together without a raging war going on,' Mr Black remarked.

'But we're 'oops, 'ir … Mista. We been lookin' for the enemy!' one of the youngsters piped in.

Mr Black looked towards the children, trying to work out who had spoken, all the while trying to decipher what had been said. Giving up on the translation, Mr Black turned to Angie and said, 'Miss, what are they talking about, and what are 'oops?'

Angie then had to go into a lengthy story of the troops and the enemy. Mr Black couldn't contain his laughter as the troops crowded around him.

'Bleedin' miracle, that's all I can say to you three, bleedin' miracle,' he said as he closed the door behind him on his way back to his unit.

Chapter 43

Bruce Evans and Sergeant Brothers were just walking in the front door of the police station when they heard One Tree Station on the air. Sergeant Brothers silently noted that he'd love to try and have a word or two to that station about listening in all the time and taking up air space on the only communication facility that was deemed reliable in the outback.

'Jimmy? Jimmy, are you there?'

'Yes, Sarge. Ronnie and I have been chatting over a coffee or two.'

Bruce quickly jumped in. 'And what have you learnt? I hope it's something useful because it seems the pilot and plane have gotten clean away.'

'Yeah, but we did get a small amount from the truck driver. It may or may not lead us to a clue, but here's hoping.' Sergeant Brothers sighed.

All four men felt very defeated, mainly for different reasons, as they sat in the main office of the police station.

'One Tree to police base, One Tree to—'

Sergeant Brothers was extremely annoyed by the radio signal so much that he was almost ready to blast One Tree and tell him not to call again.

'Yes, One Tree?'

'Oh, Sergeant Brothers. Have I got something for you—'

'Okay, One Tree!'

'Well, I was doing me usual trek to the back paddock, and youse would never guess what I found—'

'What, One Tree? What did you find?'

'One badly 'urt pilot and a plane sittin' neat as a pin in the middle of the paddock.'

'One Tree. How bad is the pilot? Is he awake? Has he spoken about anything? Have you touched the plane? Can you give us the exact location of your back paddock?'

'The location's easy, but check with the flying doctor for coordinates, the paddock 'as three 'uge boulders grouped together on the southern side near a small spring.'

'Great, One Tree, but how's the pilot?'

'Broken jaw and cheekbone, I'd guess, an' somethin' not right with 'is right shoulder. So, he ain't been talking much. He was out of the plane so no, I ain't touched that neither.'

'One Tree, you've been a very great help. We'll get the doctor ready and be out soon. Is there anything you need in the way of provisions that we could bring with us?'

'Slab of beer'd go down well, and perhaps a couple of recent papers. It tends to be a bit cut off out 'ere sometimes. A carton of ciggies be nice. Now the wife's not 'ere to hound me, I 'ave a smoke when I feel like it.'

'Yeah, sure got that, One Tree. See you soon. Police out.'

Sergeant Brothers turned and faced Jimmy wondering how to phrase what he wanted to know without seeming to be as inquisitive as most people are in this spacious non-forgiving stretch of country.

'Jimmy, you've dealt with One Tree before—for godsake, what's his name? I can hardly front up to his homestead and say, "Hello, One Tree." It'd sound like I was talking to something unhuman.'

'As I recall, some of the drifters call him Billy the Beak.'

'Really? Jimmy, that's nearly as bad. In fact, it's worse.'

'No, Sarge. His name is Billy something. The Beak is because he's always sticky-beaking into things that don't concern him.'

Chapter 44

Liam was extremely anxious as the nurse turned into the corridor heading for the maternity section. His mind was ticking over at a thousand miles an hour. What was wrong with his Mam? She'd never stayed in hospital this long with any of the other kids. Mostly it was have the baby and home the next day. Now he noticed how very fast they were moving and the shade of green that was covering walls and the ceiling.

'Liam. Liam, dear, are you alright?'

'Yeah, course.'

Luckily the nurse had anticipated this nervous reaction.

'Here, Liam, take this,' she said as she handed him a bowl.

After a little while of sitting quietly, out of the way in the corridor, Liam became his normal colour and instantly wanted to know if anyone saw him and what was the matter with him.

'I think you got yourself a little worked up, but you should be okay to see your mum now.'

They went past the nurse's station and were heading towards Mrs Sims' room when Liam wanted to stop.

'Nurse, Mam is alright, isn't she? She isn't dead, is she?'

'No, Liam, of course she's not dead. What makes you think she is?'

'Well, she was in my room talking to me last night, but it wasn't 'er. It was the mam I remember from when I was really little.'

'You must have been dreaming, Liam.'

They were outside the door and Liam's heart began thumping so hard he thought everyone could hear it. The nurse noticed his change of colour again.

'Liam, listen to me. There's nothing wrong with your mother. Now, take a long deep breath, hold it, and let it out. Do that a couple of times while I see if your mum's awake.'

As she opened the door, Mrs Sims sat up in anticipation of seeing her firstborn.

'Yes, he's here. He's very anxious to see you.'

'Please, Nurse, bring him in.'

'Mam. Oh, Mam,' was all Liam got out as he clasped his arms around her neck and burst into tears. Mrs Sims did her best at trying to calm Liam, but in the end he was totally exhausted and lay there like a rag doll.

'That smell. It reminds me. Was it somewhere, or someone? Mmm … Liam come and give me another hug. That's it,' she said as her memory was jolted. 'Ronnie. Ronnie used to wear it. Said it made him feel good. Old Spice, that's what he called it.'

Liam snuggled up to his mum and she held him until he was totally calm. The nurse popped her head around the door in time to see the transformation of the little tough guy. Mrs Sims saw and motioned that she leave him there for a while.

Chapter 45

Marie had never been a person to question the decisions of others, but now she wished she'd had more time to gather information from Beth about how Anne was doing and where she had finally made her home. Had she married? Did she stay with that young man she was involved with, or was she really just helping a person in need at the time? Marie sat there pondering these thoughts over and over in her mind. She hadn't even noticed that the day was nearly at its end, until one of the cab drivers who knew Marie walked over from the taxi-rank.

'Um … S'cuse me. Hello, Marie, thought it was you.'

'Oh, hello, Kevin. I've been sitting here daydreaming, I suppose, instead of watching the time.'

'Not to worry, I'm going your way to pick up a fare and I'd be pleased if you would accept the lift home.'

'Oh, I don't know,' she said with a mischievous twinkle in her eyes. 'I tell all the children not to accept lifts in cars. But I think I'm wise enough and you're kind enough, so let's risk it.'

'Can I enquire of the subject that had you so deep in thought for most of the afternoon? It's not usual to see you sitting alone for such a long time. Does John know where you are?'

'It's his fault that I've been here.'

'Sorry. That was impolite of me.'

'Don't worry, Kevin, it's not your fault.'

'But Marie, it's just that I've admired, sometimes with envy, how perfect your married life has been with John.'

'Kevin, normally I would agree wholeheartedly, if it wasn't for his time wasting on family history. That's why I've been sitting here, trying to remember back to my school holidays spent at Marsh Flats, and as I'm no spring chicken, it's taking all my concentration.'

They got in the cab and were making their way to Marie's home when out of the blue Kevin pulled over on the side of the road, turned the engine off and reached for Marie's arm. Before he could speak, he burst out laughing.

'If only I had a camera to catch the look on your face.'

Marie was sitting there holding on to the door, becoming more anxious by the minute.

'Kevin, you've just frightened ten years off my life. Whatever made you pull over and grab my arm?'

'Look, I do apologise, but I suddenly remembered a passenger I picked up the other day and you talking about Marsh Flats brought it all flashing back. During the fruit season, my family used to follow the work. It was a great way to see the country, but I didn't get to do a lot of schooling, not that I really cared then.'

'Who was your passenger?'

'That's it, Marie. I don't know, but I thought back to my older brother's first real girlfriend. In fact, she travelled with us for quite a while. Then she met this drifter named James Hill and left after a couple of days.'

'Kevin, I, like everyone else, enjoy a chat but I really can't see where all this is leading to.'

'But, Marie, she had told my brother she used to live at Marsh Flats, and that's why I've remembered her. She looked exactly like my brother's girlfriend: she had the same red hair. I think she said that she'd just finished a degree or something and was looking forward to working with kids. She also said she'd been in an orphanage most of her childhood after her father died.'

With puzzlement clouding her face, Marie felt she had to ask, 'Would you recognise this person again or a photograph of her?'

'Oh … I suppose. But, what for, Marie?'

They drove the rest of the journey in silence, as neither knew what the outcome would unfold, if anything at all.

'Are you sure you want me to come in? I mean, seeing as that fare I was going to has cancelled and you've been gone for hours. John is most likely worried sick.'

'I can tell you now, he'll be in his room on the back veranda with his charts, names, and photos. It's become his life.'

Marie used the front door so as to not give John a warning with that squeaky gate. Dylan was in his room but called out, 'Nana, where have you been? I was worried.'

She and Kevin went out the back to confront John. It was either going to shed light or be a total failure.

'John, this is Kevin. He gave me a lift home. Could you please show him some of your photos of people from Marsh Flats?'

'That was decent of you old chap – the lift home, I mean. Now, this is the packet of Marsh Flats. Who in particular are you trying to trace?'

As Kevin skimmed through the packet, the photos made no sense to him at all until he got to the second last one. 'That's her, the passenger I told you about.'

'But, it can't be. Oh man, that woman would be in her sixties, if she's even still alive. That photo is very old.'

'But it is. I'd stake my life on it.'

'Kevin, you will stay for a bite to eat? It's nothing special, just meatloaf and vegies.'

'Thanks, Marie, but no, I must get along. Let me know what happens with your Marsh Flats jigsaw.'

Driving away, Kevin's mind was trying to recall details of his passenger, but all that came to mind was that she was a real looker, one you wouldn't mind getting to know. Perhaps if he could control his extreme shyness of females he would've at least asked her name, but his tongue always got tied up in knots.

Chapter 46

The plane was being checked for its flight out to One Tree Station. Jimmy drove the police vehicle as close as he could to the door of the plane. Sergeant Brothers busied himself shifting the provisions into a netted area in the plane. It was a good thing this area would be vacant on the return trip: the injured pilot would need to be lying down. The flying doctor who was going with them had said it would be of utmost importance to get the man on to a saline drip and something for the agony he must be in. The doctor and his nurse arrived, but only the doctor boarded the plane. The nurse reversed the vehicle and proceeded to drive back the way they'd arrived.

Evans climbed inside the small air-craft and settled himself in the seat nearest the rear exit. Brothers was surprised. 'Hey, Doc, won't the nurse be needed?'

'Not today, I can handle this one. Besides, Karen is required to help with a birth that's in progress as we speak.'

'Oh! Right then, suppose we're nearly ready for take-off,' said Brothers.

'The pilot is just handing in his flight-path plan with expected arrival and return times. Can't leave anything to chance out here. Without the flight plan it would be impossible to find us if the plane were to go down,' said Daniel.

The pilot, Wayne, entered the plane and caught the tail end of the conversation.

'I'll have no negative talk on my plane. You should know that by now, Daniel. I've never failed to deliver you and your patients back in one piece. For how many years now?'

'Okay, Wayne, you're right, as usual.'

The ground crew were now shutting the door and taking the chocks away from the wheels. The engine was straining in anticipation of becoming airborne.

'I say, Brothers, do you mind if Daniel sits up front with me? It's just that … Well, I suppose it's superstition, but we've never had a mishap with all the trips we've made together.'

Brothers began nodding his head in agreement at the same time as the voice on the radio gave permission for takeoff. He quickly sat in the seat nearest to a window and belted up. Before the plane was even in the air, he had the file out, making notes on the questions that he would be delighted to get answers to. It still puzzled him immensely as to how or why Ronnie Sims had become connected with such a band of highly trained scum of the earth. Maybe what Ronnie said was true: wrong place, wrong time, and easy money.

Wayne and Daniel had been watching the vast area below with wonderment of the colour hues and shapes of the landscape. It caught Brothers by surprise when he felt the plane begin its descent. Surely he had not been onboard for more than ten minutes? He'd become so engrossed in studying the file still sitting on his knee. Evans had not spoken a word during the trip, but now his interest was reaching fever pitch.

'Hold on, Brothers,' Daniel called. 'We're about to land on One Tree's strip, and it could be a little bumpy.'

As the pilot steadied the plane, Daniel could see a small figure on the ground madly waving his arms at the plane trying to seek attention and direct them down to him. Daniel pointed down to the lone figure. 'There he is, Billy the Beak. One day I swear he'll wave his arms off. Poor devil. It must be hell living out here all by yourself.'

The plane now made a low sweeping turn as it lined up with the landing strip. The ground was in a hurry to make contact with the little plane. Quickly, Wayne pulled the nose up. He'd not allowed enough for the crosswind. On the second attempt, it was all clear sailing. Billy was there the instant the plane stopped, eagerly awaiting contact with outsiders as well as the provisions they'd brought.

Chapter 47

Kevin was having a slack night in his taxi, but it gave him time to ponder on what Marie had said about Marsh Flats. His brother had been really taken by this girl. Perhaps if he could think of her name it would shed more light for John's family tree.

The girl had travelled with them following the fruit work. She was a hard worker, never slacked off. In fact, she wouldn't even join in with the Saturday night get-togethers. But what was her name? She was a very private person, wouldn't talk about herself or her family. In fact, when anyone spoke of family, she would find an excuse to walk away. The way she worked she must have built up a quite a tidy nest egg in the bank. Somewhere along the track, this drifter joined in their little group. Kevin remembered he didn't like him from day one; he didn't know why, he just got bad vibes. *Damn, what was her name?*

Just then, the passenger door opened.

'G'day, mate. Take me to the airport, will you?'

It was a fairly quiet ride, each lost in their own thoughts.

As they approached the airport, his passenger turned to him and said, 'It's great to be going home. I've left it too long between visits. I'm really looking forward to seeing my new niece, Anne.'

His passenger collected his case and suit bag from the boot and gave Kevin his fare, plus a nice sized tip. Kevin placed his taxi in the queue at the taxi rank. As there were lots in front, he quickly went inside the airport to grab a snack. Whilst in there, a young girl was rushing to the departure counter. Suddenly, the two things in his head became one: red hair and a name, Anne. It didn't make much sense to Kevin, but it made him think to the time when the girl with the red hair and the drifter left. It was what caused him to go to Marsh Flats many years ago. In fact, it was the one and only time he'd seen his brother lose his temper and actually get in to a really bad fight. The drifter ended up with a broken nose, but his brother lost his one true love. As soon as his shift was finished, Kevin wondered if he should ring or just go round to Marie's house, with the name that may or may not be of any help to John's family trees. His curiosity got the better of him and he drove round to Marie's. He saw John first as Marie was hanging the washing out. John thanked him but didn't react very much, whereas Marie nearly exploded with excitement.

'Marie, please, control yourself. We have a gentleman caller.'

'Yes, John, but he's my gentleman caller, and he's just opened a floodgate of memories of Marsh Flats.'

With this Marie was busy making tea and cutting fruit cake without even thinking of whether Kevin would be staying or not.

'Now that you've calmed down old girl, why hadn't you thought of Anne yourself?'

'See what I have to put up with, Kevin? That's why long marriages are a rarity these days, but luckily I have what is called selective hearing.'

Kevin could see smiles and twinkling eyes that flashed between them, as the three of them sat down at the table.

Chapter 48

The three women were having a really tough time of getting the excited troops to quieten down. Suzy was leading the others in a song – 'Mister Black ain't no monster, Mister Black ain't no monster.' It was Angie who finally put a stop to the racket by once again calling the troops together and giving each one a slice of Boston bun and a glass of milk.

'No, Suzy, sit in a circle on the floor here in the kitchen, because it's easier to clean up a small mess in a confined area.'

'Wha' ya mean, Angie?' one of the boys asked.

'Sorry, troops. If we all sit close together the crumbs can't get far away and we don't want the enemy to start again.'

There was puzzlement on all the little faces before they all started nodding in agreement. Peace reigned for a short time. Once the food and milk was finished, the kids made excuses about leaving the kitchen. Angie, Helen, and Barbara were now able to begin assessing what welfare might decide to do with the children.

'Surely they wouldn't remove the children. I mean, we are coping, even if it seems a bit chaotic at times. Even Mr Black approves of what we've achieved – his words, "bleeding miracle".'

'You're right there, Angie. If only I were finishing my social work degree like you have.'

'Don't put yourself down, Barbara, you're doing just fine. I was just lucky to be in the right place and time to get all my practical work done in one hit.'

'Angie, what do you think you'll do? I mean, when Mrs Sims is home again.'

'Let's just say I have made a few minor plans that I'm not able to discuss just yet.'

'There you go again, Angie,' Helen chipped in.

'Is it something to do with Officer Cook?'

'No!' Angie quickly bit back, unable to hide her embarrassment under the close scrutiny of her friends. Barbara and Helen realised once again they'd pushed the wrong button and thought it best to close the subject altogether.

'Ang, you won't mind if Barbara and I duck out for a while? I mean, full-on kids are hard to cope with for an extended time. You should have seen what they got up to at the police station.'

'Sure. Look, I'm sorry I snapped.'

'It's okay, Angie. We'll see you shortly. Can we get anything for you while we're out?'

'No, thanks. I think I'll give Di a ring and see how things are progressing with Mrs Sims and Liam.'

Chapter 49

'Hello, Jill, it's Paul. Paul Hill. I was hoping you would be kind enough to accept my offer of dinner tonight.'

Jill was taken aback with the request and hoped Paul did not hear her sudden intake of breath.

'It's a small way of payment for the time you spent answering all my questions.'

'Oh, Paul, I'd love to, but it really isn't necessary, you don't owe me anything.'

'Shall I pick you up 'round 7.30? By the way, do you like seafood? There is a great new place, opened only a few weeks ago, next door to Maxine's Coffee Lounge.'

Paul realised he sounded just like a teenager on his first serious date, but in his mind, wasn't it just that medicine had had its place in his life? It never gave him the warm friendship feeling that flowed forth from Jill like a fountain of youth.

'Paul, it has been ages since I've eaten fish. It never tastes as good when you have prepared and cooked it yourself.'

As Jill hung the phone up she felt tingly all over. It had been a long time since she felt an excitement like this. Then she looked at the time. *Oh dear, I've only got two hours before Paul will be here.* Her first reaction was to reach for the CD player and pop in her favourite relaxation disc. As she was running the bath, she dropped a lavender bath bomb into the water because the thought might calm her nerves down just a bit.

Then came the dilemma of what to wear. She didn't want to overdress, but then she didn't want to underdress either. Oh! The male population have it so easy: dark pair of trousers, casual shoes, shirt and jacket, then they were ready for any occasion.

The doorbell rang. Jill took one step towards the door and then the phone screeched. She quickly let Paul in whilst reaching for the phone with her other hand.

'Sorry, Paul,' she mouthed with her hand over the phone. Jill hadn't been listening very long when Paul noticed her face blanch. Now he was in a quandary as to whether to step in or not.

'Bruce, when are you heading down south? I mean there's someone here with me right now that probably would like to speak to you about Mrs Sims' son, Liam,' Jill said anxiously.

'There is! Who, for God's sake?

'Bruce, you watch your language. It's Doctor Paul Hill, and I think now is a good time for you to talk to him.' Jill passed the phone over to Dr Hill, again mouthing, 'sorry, Paul' as she did.

'Hello, this is Dr Paul Hill speaking,' Paul said tentatively.

'Hello Dr Hill, it's Bruce Evans here. Why are you at my mother's home, and why the questions about Ronnie Sims?'

'It's not Ronnie I'm interested in, it's Liam. Why am I at your mothers? We're going out for dinner. I would like very much to meet you on your next visit to your mother's.'

'Likewise, Hill, likewise.'

After a few short minutes Paul and Bruce had managed to clarify a few more of the Sims' details that they each needed, then as quick as they were introduced, the conversation ended.

'Oh, Paul, I do hope this hasn't ruined our night out, I was so looking forward to it,' said Jill, after Paul had put down the phone.

'Then, my dear, we'll forget the phone ever rang. In fact, I can't remember hearing it ring.'

'Thank you, Paul. I'd like you to meet Bruce someday, but not today. He seemed quite stressed about something.'

'Shall we go, Jill?'

As Jill turned at the door, she wondered if she would be able to turn off her thoughts from the phone call as easily as she now turned off the lights.

Chapter 50

Di had imagined it would be relatively simple to open her home to a family that would be able to use the spaciousness of it, but what she was confronted with was piles of red tape and enough documents to start a library. It was almost enough for her to reverse the decision she'd made.

'Hello, Di, it's Angie.'

Angie heard the muffled tears that now turned into sobs.

'Di, what is it? What's the matter?'

More sobbing. Angie was really worried.

'I'll be over in two shakes, Di. Whatever the matter is, it can't be so hard that the both of us can't beat it.'

Before she had time to move, the phone rang. Her thoughts went immediately back to Di but the voice shocked her.

'Um ... Yeah ... I mean, yes, Officer Cook, it is Angie Dickson.'

'Angie, please, the name's Tim.'

'Sorry, Tim. It's just you caught me at a very bad moment.'

'What do you mean, Angie?'

'You remember Di Brown, my friend with the large family home? Well, something is not right. I just called her a moment ago and she couldn't talk for crying. In fact, I was just heading over there when you rang, that's why the strange voice. I thought it was Di ringing back.'

Then there was a passage of silence except for the busy working noise of the police station. Angie was becoming more jittery by the moment, to the point of almost hanging up.

'Angie? Sorry, Angie, I had to pass something past my super. Do you think you could wait and we'll see Di Brown together? You take your car and I'll use one of the police vehicles.'

'Look, Tim, you're frightening me with all these cloak and dagger happenings.'

'See you real soon, Angie. Bye.'

'How dare he do this to me!' she shouted to herself as she gathered her bag and mobile. By the time she got to her car, she had calmed down a lot, but now worry took its place. As Angie put her key in the car door, she realised how shot her nerves were. Her hands were shaking so much it took a couple of times before it finally opened. Once inside the car, she held the steering wheel with both hands before even turning the engine on.

This time, driving in the streets where Di lived didn't give her the same feeling of peacefulness it always had before. Officer Cook was already outside Di's address. Angie's thoughts were running riot. *Does he have to be so good looking? It's not just the uniform, but that leather jacket fits to perfection. Oh no, now that beaming smile.*

He held the door open for her and in her fluster she dropped her bag. Then bang, two heads collided. Now the whole street seemed full of apologies.

'You okay, Angie?'

'Yes, thank you, it was stupid of me to drop my bag.'

'Don't say that, you could never be stupid.'

Angie's face lit up with such red warmth that she felt she was outshining the sun.

'Could we please go and see Di? I'm really worried about my friend.'

'Sure. I'll just get a few papers my super asked me to bring for Mrs Brown to look at.'

Together they began walking down the drive, because Angie remembered Di had already shifted herself into the granny flat at the end of the garden.

'It would make a marvellous place to bring up a bunch of kids, wouldn't it?'

'What do you mean, Tim?'

'Nothing, I was just thinking out loud.'

Di opened the door and almost fell into the comfort of Angie's outstretched arms. Officer Cook stood back and watched with embarrassment, then he realised it was probably more with envy. How he wished he could be held and to be holding Angie like that.

Chapter 51

'You did a great job, Billy, I mean, to even think that the plane may not have got clean away.'

'It weren't nothing at all, Brothers. Are you going to check the pilot or the plane first?'

'I think the Doc will check out the pilot while Detective Evans and I check the plane and its cargo, or lack of it.'

'Cargo? What sort of cargo? I didn't—'

'Hell, Billy. Tell me you didn't mess with the plane.'

'No … well, not really. I jus' thought there might have been a drop of drink on board. But no such luck.'

Brothers and Evans began their walk to the plane, hoping Billy the Beak had not disturbed any vital evidence.

'Brothers,' Billy called out, 'can I get my provisions out of your plane?'

'Yes, Billy. Then sit in the shade near your truck. There may be things we need to ask you.'

'Brothers, what do people like Billy do, you know, without human company, while they farm or manage these properties?'

'It seems hard for them not to be here. The properties are handed down and next year is always going to be the best history has ever seen. But in the meantime, they scratch out a living by shifting their animals from here to there just to keep them alive.'

'I'm sure I couldn't hack it. Even my time in the Middle East was a picnic compared to some of the country out here.'

They now turned their attention to the plane.

'Where do we start?'

'Not in the most obvious place. They're experts in hiding things in places you'd never dream of.'

After hours of searching, it looked as hopeless as it could. But then Evans' mind began to niggle away.

'Brothers, I think we need to have a word or two with Billy.'

'Why? What could he tell us?'

'Don't know yet. But I have a hunch and they've never let me down before.'

Billy saw them walking back empty-handed and the perspiration began pouring down his back, soaking his shirt.

'Hey, Billy, must be a lot hotter in the shade by the look of your shirt.'

'Sergeant Brothers, I didn't think it would do no 'arm. I mean why do planes 'ave to carry so many spare tyres? I jus' thought I might be able to flog 'em off next time I was in town.'

'Spare tyres?' both men said in unison.

'Yeah. Six of 'em,' said Billy.

'Where are they now, Billy?'

'I put them in the feed-shed near the house.'

'You're sure of that? There is nothing else you haven't mentioned in there?' asked Evans.

'Brothers, I'll go back to the house with Billy to retrieve the cargo. Try to get Jimmy on the radio. I think your guest and I will be making a trip to the big smoke, as soon as I tie up a few loose ends.'

'Okay, Evans, but will you be back here before nightfall? With the flying doc gone already, I mean, I don't like the outback at night when it's me who'll be alone. I must have been listening to too many of Jimmy's spirit stories.'

Chapter 52

Marie had been very unsettled since that chance encounter with Kevin. Surely his older brother had not met Anne? The time and ages just did not seem right. It would dent her pride to ask, but there was no other way to begin to find answers.

'John. John, dear, can I ask you a few questions about Marsh Flats?'

'Music to my ears,' John teased.

'No, John, none of your tomfoolery. This is special. I need to know how Kevin thought his older brother met and was head over heels in love with Anne's daughter.'

'Wait a tick while I get that relevant chart. Here, let's see if we can unravel a few mysteries.'

'John, however do you collect all these names and dates?'

'Elementary, my dear Watson, elementary! First, the local councils hold an ample supply, then there's the library, and after that personal contact. Here we are. Anne Simmonds who married James Hill. You're quite right about the time factor. Anne's daughter Fay would seem far too old. That is, unless therein lies a family skeleton.'

'John, you can't think that. I know Anne was a disappointment to her parents when she up and left so soon after the death of her brother. You know, John, I didn't even know Anne had ever gotten married.'

'Leave it with me for a while, Marie. I'll need time to check my records and possibly make some use of the library.'

'Thanks, John. I thought I might go and visit with Mrs Sims, check on Liam, and of course see the new babies.'

'Now, don't you go getting clucky on me, old girl!'

'Really, John, you come out with outlandish things sometimes.'

'But, it's the truth. You love new babies, whoever's child they are.'

Marie turned and left John to his muttering and shifting papers from one side to another, jotting down little snippets here and there.

Marie went to catch the bus for the trip in to visit the hospital and the Sims. As she sat on the bus heading towards town, her thoughts were elsewhere, and Marie almost forgot to get off at the stop near the hospital. It only happened because she had to move to let the man out that was sitting beside her.

'Oh! I'm sorry. I was miles away. This is my stop also.'

This was not a good start. She wanted to be calm and clearheaded when she met Mrs Sims, because somehow she had to try and get some family information from her without it seeming like an interrogation. Marie knocked and entered in one movement, and what she saw dumbfounded her. Hadn't everyone commented on the size of this woman?

'Mrs Sims, hello, I'm Marie, Dylan's grandmother.'

Now the ice was broken, could she keep up the conversation? 'I've been meaning to come by and see you, but there never seems enough hours in the day. I hope you got the pot plant I left with the staff for you.'

Leila was nodding in agreement. Marie thought now was the time to bite the bullet.

'Have your parents seen the babies yet? I suppose Mr Sims is quite proud and feeling on top of the moon.'

Leila's hand reached for Marie's. Now, both women were wrapped in each other's embrace, sharing the joy of motherhood. Then Marie became a little concerned at the state Leila had worked herself into.

'Mrs Sims, I'm really sorry if I've said something wrong.'

Now Leila was shaking her head as she dried her tear-stained face.

'It's a long story, but I can't tell you because I don't know where on earth to begin.'

At this chance, Marie jumped in boots and all, because she felt it was now or never to obtain information about Leila's parents. Perhaps it was a bit much pride on both sides that had kept them apart and away from their grandchildren.

'Can I at least phone your parents? With the shock of looking death in the face, surely they'll come and see you, won't they?'

'Marie ... it's been such a long time. I disappointed my father very much ... I don't think he would come.'

'At least let me try – there is no harm in trying. How do you spell your father's name and whereabouts do they live?'

'As far as I know, they have never moved from the house that I lived in. His name is spelt T-A-N-E-K-A-H-A. Yes, I know, it's a mouthful and I used to be teased at school all the time.'

Chapter 53

'Oh, excuse my manners, Di, this is Officer Tim Cook.'
'Nothing to excuse, just wish I was thirty or so years younger.'

Now both Tim and Angie turned a bright shade of red.

'Come on, you two, before you both melt on the spot. Come inside.'

Di insisted they at least have coffee with her while she began telling them about the red tape and duplication that keeps local government in local knowledge, or maybe lack of it. There was nothing Angie or Tim could do to change the subject. It was as though a tap had been turned on and there was no way of turning it off. Tim had seen this many times during his service with the police. He sometimes thought that government departments didn't really know what they needed from clients, so they just made the wording smaller and more complex so that older clients just gave up and never went ahead with the venture they had started with, thus ending many worthwhile projects. It was Tim's movement to put their cups on the sink that caused Di to take a breath.

'Oh, Angie, why on earth didn't you stop me? I mean, I've been rambling on, not even giving a moment's notice to what you both have come to see me about.'

Angie looked at Tim. He in turn looked at Di.

'Aw, come on, one of you, please. Say what you have to say. I suppose it's got something to do with my plans?'

'Yes, Di, it has, but I'll let Tim tell you.'

'I should have known. Neighbours complaining about the noise, before it even begins. No. Wait a minute. They shouldn't even know about my plans yet.'

'That's right, Di. No one knows anything. My super asked if I could show you these papers, and I'll explain anything that is a mystery to you.'

'Angie, does this mean what I think it does?' asked Di, as her voice caught in the back of her throat.

All Angie could do was nod her head, because she too felt if she spoke the tears would fall before she uttered a sound. It was up to Tim now to take charge of the situation.

'Ladies, could I have your utmost attention whilst I read through the necessary details. My super has condensed it so it's quite understandable.'

By the time he'd finished, Di was smiling as she saw now that her plan would come to fruition and there'd be no more red tape, jargon, or even departments to deal with. Except, of course, the welfare keeping their hand in on behalf of the children, and Di could handle that, no worries.

'But, hold on ladies. What if the parents aren't willing to accept the move and, may I say, extreme generosity on your part Di?'

'I know they will.' Di beamed. 'I know they will.'

'But, how? I hope you haven't mentioned this to anyone other than yourself, Angie, Helen, and Barbara?'

'No, it's my inner feelings and they have never let me down before.'

'I'd love to stay chatting with both of you, but now the papers are signed I need to start the wheels in motion.'

'You mean it is really going to happen?'

'Yes, and when I need a fairy godmother, I hope it will be you standing behind me.'

Tim stood gathering the papers together and made a quicker than normal departure without even looking back at Angie.

'Gee, Angie, he is a really nice young man.'

'Really, Di, does everyone think they have to organise my love life—I mean, my life?'

Di now had Angie in her arms thinking back to when she had met her soul mate and she let him go because she had felt pressured by well-meaning friends. It took years after that before she met Donald. They had spent many, many happy years of marriage, but there was, in Di's mind, just a little something missing. But it was no good trying to change the past.

'Di, I must go. You know, places to be, things to do.'

Angie and Di walked up the long driveway towards the main street. Angie quickly opened the gate and closed it behind her.

'Bye, Di,' was all she could manage without crying. Now, driving along she began telling herself off for being too sentimental.

Chapter 54

'One Tree Station to police base, One Tree—'
'Okay, already, One Tree, I thought you'd been warned not to use this air-space unless it was of utmost importance?'

'Great, Jimmy, at least someone is following orders.'

'One Tree Station, who is this? Please, One Tree.'

'It's okay, Jimmy, it's Bruce Evans. Could you please get our visitor showered, shaved and changed? We're leaving for the big smoke at the first available flight.'

'Does that mean—no, sorry, no questions over the air.'

'See you soon, Jimmy.'

Evans walked around the homestead with Billy, looking at what was once a proud and majestic building. Veranda on all four sides of the house, wooden shutters beside each window, although now hanging at odd angles. At one time, someone had loved this house; there were the remnants of wisteria along the railings, a hoya plant still surviving as it attached itself securely to the wall on the southern side. As they walked through the house, Bruce was astonished to think that a man could live in this condition voluntarily, but then, as Brothers had said, what other choice do they have apart from shutting the door and walking away from something handed down over three or four generations? Between the back of the house and the feed shed there were still the remains of a kitchen garden; herbs of all sorts, and flagstones that still marked out pathways between the once prosperous vegetable patches. He was surprised to find a couple of stunted fruit trees, still holding their mummified fruits.

'Do you never think of starting the garden again?'

'What's the point? You get something growing nicely then along comes a really wet year or such a hot wind that everything cooks in the ground. Every drop of moisture I need is for the stock. I've even seen the chooks drop dead as they walk across the ground. In fact, that was the last straw when the missus had a clutch of chickens die because the hen didn't make it back to the nest before the crow found them.'

'But, why don't you just leave?'

'Mate, the bank owns me to my hairline. At least while I'm still making a scratch they don't hound me to death.'

'Let's go take a bo-peep at your tyres.'

'Ah … yeah. Look, Brothers, I might have taken just a bit more than tyres …'

Chapter 55

Marie had never had the mind of a super-sleuth like her husband, but she was sure if there was a way of getting around this problem, she would find it. Maybe she could get in touch with some of the community members of the Pacific Island group that she knew met monthly in the library. Marie worried about how to ask delicate questions without seeming nosy into matters and people she didn't know. Marie's mind was now very weighed down. *Perhaps I'll have to seek help from John.* At this point, she began to analyse why she was thinking like this. Hadn't she told Mrs Sims that she'd try to locate her father and let him know about the babies and Leila's close call with death? The local library was the base to start because of their notice board that had everything covered from A to Z. As luck would have it, there was a meeting for Pacific Islanders and friends next week. So then Marie would have only three days to gather thoughts together and write down the questions she hoped could shed a little light on to Leila's family. As the bus pulled away from the curb, Marie could see John was watering the front lawn.

'Hey, where've you been?'

'Just to the library, John. Why? What's the matter?'

'Nothing. It was just that Dylan wanted to go to the hospital to see Liam.'

'And tomorrow is Saturday. Why don't we ring and see if Liam could come and spend a few hours here?'

'There … I knew it woman. That's what you've been planning all along. You just took a little longer than I thought you would.'

Marie was about to tell John his fortune when she caught sight of the beaming face of her grandson standing in the front porch.

'Oh … Nana, can we? Grandy, please can he come, just for a little while?'

Dylan was holding the door open for his grandparents when suddenly John swung around.

'Marie, where is your library bag and books? Didn't leave it on the bus again?'

Marie felt the flush starting at her throat as it raced to her eyebrows. Her mind was working overtime to come up with an answer that John would leave alone for the present. Now was not the time to discuss Liam's family.

'Dylan, could you be an angel and go put the kettle on? Oh, take this too, it's a special treat for us to have for afternoon tea.'

'Now, that was a well-planned tactical move, I must say. What was that for? You're planning something else, aren't you?'

'Oh John … not really … but I did tell Leila I would try and make contact with her parents for her.'

'You what?' John blustered. 'You'll never know where to start.'

'But you're wrong … I'm going to a meeting on Monday. So I was going to ask you to take Dylan to his physio appointment and also give me some questions to ask that are not going to be deemed intrusive.'

'My wife – the super sleuth. Good on you for giving it a go. Now, let's go see what treat you've bought for afternoon tea.'

Chapter 56

Di and Officer Cook sometimes thought they were in an old fashioned child's game of paper chase. During the past ten days, Di could feel things were finally drawing to a close. The biggest hurdle had been left to last. Not because she was afraid, but more so anxious as to how the news would be given and how it would be received. Putting all this behind her, she now thought again about how happy Angie looked in the presence of the police officer. It was about time that Angie began giving herself a bit of freedom to enjoy life. Thinking about enjoying life, the image of Liam, his mum, and the twins flashed into her brain. Yes, it was the weekend tomorrow and she'd made her mind up that she would visit all four. During the night, Di had the strangest dreams that wove in and out of the past, present, and future. As she was watching Liam grow tall and strong along with his brothers and sisters, she also watched in amazement as Leila regained some of what must have been the attraction that captivated young Ronnie. Early morning sun was peeking around the edges of the window blind. Di stirred as her cat began taking tentative steps towards the pillow, purring as he moved.

'Come on, come on. Yes, I'm waking up now, you old rascal. Oh Puss, I wish sometimes you could speak because I had such wonderful dreams last night. I just hope it was really a glimpse of the future.'

Di and her cat did their morning ritual, stroking down the back, massage the head and neck, now straight on to his back for the best delight – tummy rubs and tickles. After all this attention, breakfast was least thing Puss thought of. He now watched through narrow slits as Di moved towards the bathroom, but he was too content to go out and wait in the kitchen for his breakfast. This, of course, changed the instant he heard Di coming back into the bedroom. He was still stretching his full length in the patch of sunlight at the end of the bed.

'Come on, lazy bones, breakfast time.'

This, of course, was his signal to move – he always liked to be first into the kitchen.

Chapter 57

'Billy, if you've wrecked my only chance of nailing some of the scum I deal with, you will have me on your back for the rest of your days.'

Evans was striding towards the feed shed as Billy slunk along like a child who'd been caught out. Evans was so annoyed that when he reached the door he pulled a touch too hard and the door departed from its hinges, crashing down and throwing up a dust cloud that obliterated everything from sight momentarily.

'Geez, Evans. Did ya hav'ta?'

'Shut it, Billy. Now, where are the souvenirs that you took from the plane?'

'Hey! I want to know what ya goin' to do with me first.'

'Look, Billy. I'm sorry for snapping but this could be the break we've been waiting for to nail these people.'

'Yeah, okay. Over there, see where the bales are piled up on that blue tarpaulin? Well, it's under the tarp in sealed up boxes and the tyres are over there near me tractor.'

Billy went and brought the ute up close to the feed shed door. They both loaded everything that had been on the plane. Evans was mindful of the time. He wanted to get back to Brothers and also to organise their flight back to the police station. As he sat in the ute, he hoped that Brothers' radio was in a reception area. If not, he'd just have to radio Jimmy to organise a plane.

'Gee, Evans, am I glad to hear your voice.'

'Okay, already. I need a plane out of here pronto.'

'Just for a couple of spare tyres, I don't think so. I thought we'd take them in Billy's ute.'

'Let's just say Billy has made a substantial donation to the territory police force. You can do the organising with Jimmy from there, correct?'

'Yes, sir. Yes, Evans. I'll be glad to see you both. The shadows were beginning to play tricks with my mind as well as my eyes. See ya.'

Brothers had to walk around a bit 'til he found a good reception area.

'Jimmy. Jimmy, do you hear me? Jimmy!'

'Is that you, Sergeant Brothers?'

'Yes. Evans wants you to organise a plane out here now. Yeah, I know the time, we'll have to light a few fires and use Billy's spotlights on his ute.'

'All this for a few tyres!'

'Um … Well, Billy has made some sort of donation to us that needs to be collected immediately, if not sooner.'

Jimmy jumped on the phone to the only pilot he knew that would fly out to that area at this time of night.

'Police base calling Sergeant Brothers. Police base—'

'Great, Jimmy. I hope I'm going to like your answer.'

'Yes, Sarge. Tony Johnson is just juicing up his plane. He will call you when he's getting close so that you can light your fires.'

'I'll owe you one for this, Jimmy. Maybe we'll organise a BBQ for everyone involved in this.'

'Everyone! Yes, even our guest Ronnie.'

It was quite late and black as pitch when the plane finally returned to the airport. Rather than move all of the load again tonight, Evans and Brothers decided they would sleep on the plane, just to be on the safe side. Tony took Billy back to his place. Billy was given strict orders from Evans that if he even whispered a word tonight, he'd end up in the cells – never to be released.

Chapter 58

Kevin was cruising around in his taxi. The streets were busy with traffic, but it made more sense to be out looking for a customer rather than sitting idly on a rank waiting for someone to open the door, or to have that nice young radio operator interrupt your thoughts by reeling off the address of a client. Kevin's mind was a thousand miles away, when almost by automatic response, he slammed his brakes on just a touch too hard. The squeal of the tyres on the road caused the pedestrians to snap their heads in his direction as if it was done on a parade-ground command. Feeling rather silly and looking very embarrassed, he averted his eyes from their stares of indignation. Then he saw her; it had to be. Her face had been engraved into his brain, but the flame red hair was no longer visible. As the lights changed he watched as she went into a cafe on the corner. Quickly, he snatched his mike from the cradle on the dashboard.

'74 to base. 74 to base.'

'Yes, Kevin, what's your problem?'

'Nothing. I'm just letting you know I'll be off the air for a while. I'm taking a coffee break.'

Things were looking promising as there was a vacant two-hour meter just round the corner, but Kevin was getting the jitters again. He walked back and past the cafe to make sure she had gone in. To his frustration she still had that close fitting beanie on and she was side on to the window. What had Marie told him? Take three deep breaths and blow each one out. He really could feel that he was calming. All he had to do was open the door and casually look around before attracting the attention of the waitress. Now his mind was racing. *What do I say to her? Remember me, I was your taxi driver a while back when I took you to the airport? Did you have a nice holiday? Do you mind if I sit at your table?* Kevin slowly walked towards her table, willing his knees to stop shaking and hoping that he would be able to speak to her.

'Excuse me, would you mind if I sit at your table? I do hate sitting alone.'

She looked up quickly, with a startled look that passed as though she knew she'd seen this person before but couldn't bring to mind where.

'Sure, I'll just move my bag. Um … Do I know you from somewhere?'

'Ah … No … Ah, I drove you to the airport.'

'Oh, of course, now I remember. My name is Barbara.'

'Pleased to meet you. I'm Kevin.'

After two cups of coffee they were getting along like two long-lost friends.

'Look, I have to be getting back on the road, but I would really like to take you out for dinner. Are you free Sunday night? I'd really rather it was tomorrow night, but that is the busiest night of the week for a cab driver.'

'Kevin. Um …'

Now he thought he'd blown it. Maybe dinner was too strong to start with; maybe he should have just chosen another coffee chat.

'Yes, Kevin, I'd love to. I'll write my address down for you. See you about eight o'clock.'

Kevin felt as though he floated back to his taxi.

'74 to base, 74 to base.'

'Yes, Kevin, you're back. Hey, you didn't have anything stronger than coffee, did you? You sound strange, you okay?'

'Never better, base. Isn't the world wonderful?' he said as he hung the mike back in its cradle.

Chapter 59

Saturday morning and Dylan was up and washed, quite a bit earlier than normal. He was very anxious that everything would work out well today. Now, he worried maybe Liam wouldn't want to come and if he did, would he like his grandparents' home? It was on the ground, not like Liam's high up above the city. Dylan was standing before the kitchen window, lost in a world of his own, and didn't hear Marie until she put her arm around him.

'Oh, sorry, Dylan. I didn't mean to startle you.'

'You didn't, Nana. I was just thinking of Liam. What if he doesn't want to come here?'

'Why would he not want to, darling?'

'Well, he lives in a unit that's high above everything, maybe he won't like it here in the flat.'

Marie hung on to this notion while she tried to digest the information her grandson had just said.

'Er … How about you help me prepare breakfast?'

'Sure, Nana.'

He didn't say anything more but Marie could see his mind was still whirling around.

'Where's Grandy?'

'He left a while back to collect Liam, so that we could all have your favourite breakfast together.'

'You mean stacks of pancakes with syrup? How do you know Liam will come?'

Marie said, 'I rang the hospital last night, while you and Grandy were watching the video, and asked Liam myself.'

'Oh, Nana, thank you. It will be great to see him again. When is he going to leave the hospital for good?'

'Soon, dear, very soon.'

Now the two were bustling round the kitchen preparing for what Dylan thought of as the most wonderful meal that his grandmother could ever have thought to make for Liam. They both heard the gate squeak. Dylan immediately thought that coming in the back door meant Liam wasn't coming because Grandy would have used the front door for a first time guest. Grandy came in alone. This was too much for Dylan who put his head down searching for a handkerchief in one of the pockets of his cage to quell the tears gathering in his eyes.

'Geez ... ya not sooking again, are ya?' Liam said with a cheeky grin as he rounded the corner of the house.

Now there was deathly silence as the two boys eyed each other off. There again flashed the secret adult signals that neither of the boys saw.

'Well, Liam. Hope you like pancakes for breakfast!'

'Yeah, well ... um. I thought we'd be havin' it here, but I don't mind goin' to McDonalds with ya.'

The instant laughter had to be explained to the dumbfounded Liam.

'Oh sure, Dilly. Like me Mam makes.'

'You can help if you'd like to. I'll show you how I try to turn them without breaking them.'

The pancakes seemed non-ending. Marie was glad she had made lots of extra batter.

'Geez, Mrs Hunter, them pancakes was beaut. Dilly, I'm too stuffed ta move.'

'Nana, is it okay if we clean up later? I'd like to show Dylan around the house.'

'Sure, boys, off you go.'

'Wow ... That's some television. I mean, it's nearly as big as me dad's.'

The two boys now went into every nook and cranny that was in the house. They thought they'd look outside. Passing Grandy's papers, Liam saw the same photo that had caused Dylan such grief.

'Hey ... Watcha doin' with me photo?' he said. As he reached towards it Grandy got there first.

'Hold on, my boy.'

'I'm not ya boy,' shouted Liam.

'No, you're not. Now come over here and have a really good look at it. See anything that seems a bit strange?'

Liam frowned as he studied the photo.

'Well, it looks like me, but me hairs different and I'd never wear gear like that. Who is it?'

'That's my ... It's what I'm working on finding out, but I think I already know now.'

As the boys checked out the garden and backyard Liam seemed amazed at the things that were there. To cover himself he kept saying that his dad had a garden 'just like this.' But in his mind he couldn't believe that the things he thought only came from shops really grew in people's gardens. Only he'd never be able to grow things – not living in his concrete jungle.

Chapter 60

Di had arrived at the hospital around mid-morning. Having enquired after Liam, she was delighted to be told he'd gone out for the day with the Hunters. *Oh well,* she thought. *That will give me more time alone with Leila and the babies.* As she left the elevator and began heading for Leila's room, a thought rushed through her head that caused an abrupt stop. The nurse walking in the same direction, whilst studying the chart she was carrying, nearly bowled Di over.

'Oh, look, I'm so sorry. I wasn't looking.'

'No, no, it's my fault. I shouldn't have stopped like that. It's just I had a horrible thought that I'd left something rather important at home.'

Di was now searching through her bag getting more worried by the moment. She was sure she'd put them in there last night.

'Can I be of any help? You know, two heads are sometimes better than one.'

'Well, I had or thought I had put an envelope of photos in here to show Leila Sims.'

'That's easy fixed.'

Di almost shouted at the nurse, thinking she'd say, 'Just go home again and get them.'

'Look in your jacket pocket. I can see part of the yellow envelope sticking out.'

'Oh. Thank you. You must think I'm a silly old fool.'

'Nothing of the sort. I'm sure Mrs Sims will enjoy a visit. Do you know her well?'

'No … not really. I'm a teacher at her son's school.'

'Enjoy your visit. Bye, now.'

Di arrived at Leila's door, feeling uncomfortable at being so flustered. She decided it would be best to stay outside a few minutes to regain her composure. Although, this was not to be as the door opened, and before Di could say anything the ward cleaner announced there was a visitor.

'Hello, Mrs Sims.'

'Um … Oh, hello, Mrs Brown.'

Di then reached out for the chair to bring it closer to the bed where it would be more comfortable talking from.

'Mrs … ah … Di, have you heard? I'll be leaving this place next week and so will Liam. I should be really happy but—'

'Is there something wrong, Leila? It's not the babies, is it?'

'No, they're growing every day. I had a person from the child welfare department drop in.' As Leila said this, tears welled up in her beautiful, large, dark eyes.

'Do they have a problem with you or the kids?'

Reaching for a tissue to stop the flow of tears she said, 'No … It's just … well, we can't stay in the unit anymore.'

Now, there was a torrent of tears as well as sobbing. Di put her arms around Leila and held her till she was calm again.

'What did they say exactly? They must have told you something?'

'They did. But I don't really understand just what they meant.'

'Why not? Maybe I can help if you tell me.'

'Well. You see, they said someone – a retired teacher, I think they said – well, this person has a very large house and they said this person is willing to let us rent the house for a small rent in return for company and a few odd jobs, like doing the lawns and garden. They also said this person would be ah … um … I think it was being some sort of guardian for the family.'

'What part don't you understand, Leila?'

'This person might be horrible – maybe they hate kids and their noise. I don't know what it would be like living with a stranger, and what's meant by a guardian?'

Di retrieved the envelope of photos and set about placing them on the bed in front of Leila. Puzzlement clouded Leila's face as she looked at them.

'Leila, a guardian is someone who is willing to step in and help keep people as a family and also liaise with the welfare if any problems arise.'

Leila was still admiring the photos Di had laid out on the bed when she swung round to face Di with such a look of amazement at the sudden realisation of what she was hearing and seeing.

'Di … I …' Tears were streaming again as she reached for more tissues, but this time it was through happiness.

'Yes, Leila. If it's okay with you and your family, you will now be my tenants.'

'Pinch me, please. I think I've just died and gone to heaven. Ronnie won't believe it.'

'Will it suit you if your belongings are moved with the children the day you come out of hospital? You know, making a fresh start with the new babies?'

'That would be wonderful, but what about Ronnie? You only said the children. I can't do it if he's not welcome as well.'

Chapter 61

Jimmy arrived at work to find his boss had not returned last night, because the phone message was still sticky-tapped to the phone. Doubts and worry were clouding his thinking. He paced around the office trying to think which direction he should start looking. Should he start by making phone calls? Should he drive to the airport before trying to raise Tony Johnson? Should he try to radio the plane? Before Jimmy had time to make a decision, the phone rang.

'Hello, police, Constable Jim—'

'Hi, Jimmy, it's Brothers. Could you bring the paddy wagon out to the plane?'

'Oh ... I'm so glad to hear your voice, Sarge.'

'Yes, yes. Just don't take too long, Jimmy.'

As Jimmy drove, his mind was filling with all sorts of reasons as to why Sergeant Brothers was at the plane now. He hadn't mentioned Evans or even Tony Johnson. What could possibly have gone wrong?

Brothers heard the vehicle and opened the plane door, shading his eyes from the blinding light.

'Gee, Sarge. You look terrible.'

'Thanks, Jimmy. This plane's sleeping quarters are not the most comfortable.'

'But, why stay here?'

'Jimmy, just back up the wagon to the door. We've got some cargo to shift, pronto.'

'But I thought—'

'Yeah, it doesn't pay to think sometimes.'

Jimmy's eyes nearly popped out of his head when he saw the amount of cargo. He'd been under the impression that it was only a few spare tyres.

'How's our guest, Jimmy?'

'Fine, Sarge. The pilot is recovering nicely, too.'

'That's good. Evans will have two travelling companions.'

'Ah ... Did you mean it, Sarge? I mean, the BBQ.'

'Sure did. When can you get things organised? This evening or tomorrow would be good if you can get things moving.'

Jimmy left the police wagon as he'd already been in touch with Tony Johnson. He hadn't walked very far at all when Tony's vehicle pulled up beside him. After exchanging greetings with both Tony and Billy, the three of them set off to organise the BBQ.

'Brothers, are you sure this lot will be safe if we leave it loaded in the vehicle and lock it in the police garage?'

'Sure thing, Evans. Who would want to steal a police paddy wagon?'

Evans was sitting, quietly thinking about what had happened since his arrival in the Territory. It was almost beyond his belief that he had finally put a stop to this load from going any further. Surely this would save the lives of some young people who had not yet become addicted to the horrors of life on drugs.

'We'll need someone to plastic wrap this lot onto a pallet before its flight south,' said Sergeant Brothers.

Evans was jolted out of his daydream.

'Yeah, sure. But find someone you trust and can rely on, Brothers.'

'I know just the person.'

'Oh?' said Bruce curiously.

'Jimmy's father. He once worked in removal of furniture and museum items, when they were transferred to other museums.' The sergeant had a wealth of local knowledge.

'Sounds like just what we want. Can you get hold of him soon?' asked Bruce.

'I'll tell Jimmy to invite him to our BBQ and we can take it from there.'

'Righto. Now, I'm going to find a nice hot shower and a comfortable bed for a couple of hours. I suggest you try and do the same, Brothers.'

Evans was thinking how he'd never appreciated a hot shower as much as this, and it was great to get out of these stiff, dust encrusted clothes. He was now thinking of his mother – he must give her a call to let her know he was heading south in a couple of days, and would she mind putting him up for a couple of nights, just 'til he knew what his next assignment was? He figured it would take a couple of days just to explain to her that he had not thrown away his job with the police force, just changed situations. He must have drifted off into a deep sleep, because when the phone beside the bed began ringing, he only heard it from a great distance.

'Good evening, Detective Evans. Sergeant Brothers asked me to call and let you know your cargo is already packed and your flight with two guests is booked for Wednesday.'

'Thanks, Jimmy. Tell me, who's coming to our little farewell party?'

'The three of us, my father, Ronnie, Tony Johnson, Billy the Beak, and perhaps the flying doc. If that suits you.'

'Sounds like a good mixture. I'll bring a couple of slabs and bags of ice, if you've got something to put them in?'

'Ah ... Sarge said you were just to come, not supply.'

'Then it looks like you'll have to do some persuasive talking. And, Jimmy, I'm really looking forward to meeting your dad.'

<h1 style="text-align:center">Chapter 62</h1>

Barbara felt slightly guilty when she told Helen and Angie that they'd have to manage the tribe on their own for at least a couple of hours on Sunday evening. As she had already predicted, the interrogation began.

'What's he like?'

'No, where's he from?'

'Where does he work? Has he got family near here?'

Barbara stood there with her hands on her hips. 'Well, if you'll give me a chance I'll explain it all even though I don't think I should have to.'

Angie looked shocked because she'd never seen her friend stand up for herself before. Helen knew they'd better diffuse the situation quickly.

'Oh, Barbara. I think it's wonderful that you're going out. That means there's hope left for us yet.'

'Helen, that's a stupid statement if ever I have heard one. Hasn't Officer Tim been after Angie to go out with him?'

'Um ... Well ... We'll just have to find someone for you and we can – all of us – go out together sometime.'

'It's already sort of arranged,' Angie said. 'Tim's friend Brian would love to go out with us, once we've settled the Sims family.'

'I don't think I like having my life arranged for me,' snorted Helen. 'You could have asked me first.'

Screaming and yelling stopped all conversation for the three friends. They stood as if glued to the floor, hoping it was only one of the kids having a nightmare. Suzy tiptoed through the lounge and sought out someone who would hold her tight and make her little heart stop pounding as though it was trying to break free of her ribcage.

'Suzy. Suzy, dear, it's alright.'

Angie scooped the child into her arms.

'Suzy, you're shivering. Let's get an extra blanket for you. We don't want you catching a cold, do we?'

'I'm not really cold, Angie. It's me dad, he spoke to me, but he's not 'ere, is he?'

'No, little one, he's not. Would you like a nice warm Milo before you go back to bed?'

'But Miss … Angie, he's comin' soon. Real soon.'

Eyes flashed between the three adults, because there was something truly uncanny about Suzy. Did she really know her father was coming home? All three of them hoped he really was because with the move next week, it would be great to have him there to move in with his family, not just arrive at the unit and find it empty.

'I really like you, but I wish Mam was home,' said Suzy as she snuggled in even closer to Angie.

'I know you do, but it won't be long now. Ready for your Milo? Helen's made it already. Just between us, you can have a chocolate biscuit to go with it, but please don't tell the others because it's the last one.'

It didn't take long before Suzy's eyelids were drooping and Angie carefully carried her back to bed. She stood looking down at the elfin face lying on the pillow and hoped that all the wishes this girl could think of would someday come true.

'Sorry about the interruption Barbara, now what questions are you going to answer first? Before we tie you to the chair and commence to torture the words from your mouth.'

Barbara swung around quickly and before she had time to open her mouth, she saw that no harm was meant, only teasing. In fact, they were really interested in Kevin. What could she tell them? Because so far she didn't really know much about him herself.

'He was the driver in the taxi I took to the airport. The next time we bumped into each other was, um ... at a coffee shop when he asked if he could share my table. So, there's really nothing else I can tell you.'

Helen was quick to ask, 'Was the cafe so busy that all the other tables were occupied?'

'Um ... Well ... No, I suppose they weren't. Do you think he really just wanted to talk to me?'

In unison from the other two came a resounding, 'YES!'

Chapter 63

Having spent the most wondrous day in his short life with Dylan and his grandparents, it was now time for Liam to return to the hospital. If it was at all possible, these two young boys now had their friendship set in concrete more solidly than anyone else realised.

'Geez, Dilly, I've had a great time. Maybe when me dad's back, and we move back 'ome instead of that unit, youse can visit me.'

It was fortunate John was standing close to Marie at this moment, because his warning squeeze came at the same instant that she began to say something.

'What did you say, Nana?'

It was the look on John's face that warned her.

'Nothing dear, nothing at all.'

John was gathering bits and pieces together that Liam thought he should take back to the hospital, only he didn't know Liam had helped himself to something that at this moment was hidden in the depths of his pockets.

'Dilly, will you come and visit me when ya got the next physio?'

'Sure, Liam. I'd love to. It's okay, isn't it, Nana?'

'Yes, of course, darling.'

John was becoming a little impatient. He wanted to get Liam back to the hospital because he needed some quiet time with Marie. Even though he hated other people doing it, he thumped his hand on the horn a couple of times.

'He's not cranky with me, is he?' Liam asked.

'No, dear, but I suppose we have kept him waiting while he's already in the car.'

'Um … Okay. See ya, Dilly. I had a swell time. Ah … Er, thanks, Mrs Hunter.'

Dylan stood on the front porch and waved to his friend until he could no longer see the tail lights of the car.

'Liam is a very nice little boy once you get to really know him.'

'Oh, Nana. Don't ever say anything like that when Liam can hear you. He hates it.'

'But why? He is nice.'

'I know, but Liam has to be tough. When his dad's away, he thinks he has to be head of his family. You know, to protect them or something.'

Marie was now seeing the Sims family in a different light and it made it more important that she try and track down Leila's parents.

'Hey, Nana, what are you thinking about?'

'Oh, nothing, dear. What would you like for tea tonight?'

Dylan looked strangely at his Nana. 'Nana, we've already had tea. We had it early before Liam went back to the hospital. Are you sure you're okay?'

Marie realised how much she was worrying that she wouldn't achieve the task she'd set herself for Monday. She and John would just have to sit down quietly and work out a plan of action.

It wasn't until Sunday evening that they finally got the time they needed. Dylan had been very tired and went to bed early. It didn't seem to flow as easily as Marie had hoped; she thought John was just making it more difficult. This thought wouldn't leave her mind. So in the end she just gave up and said she didn't think she could go through with it.

'But, what about the woman, Mrs Sims, didn't you say you'd try somehow?'

'Goodnight John.'

Marie now left him to clear the papers away.

It was a restless night for both of them; neither got much sleep at all. Marie was so nervous in the morning she gave Dylan his grandfather's strong black tea, and was then really taken aback by John's response.

'Good God, woman. What do you expect me to do with Milo?'

That was the last straw. She left the kitchen sobbing.

'Grandy, what's wrong with Nana?'

'Not much. It's just how women behave when they come to what looks like an insurmountable problem.'

'But … Grandy … I'll go and see if Nana wants a hug!'

Before Dylan had even made it to the hallway, he caught a fleeting glimpse of half a coat and a handbag before the front door closed with a sharp bang.

'Grandy, Grandy. What's happening? Nana just left! Should you, I mean, are you going to?'

'No, my boy. Your Nana has hatched up this project that I wish her every success in, but I really think she's taken on a wee bit too much to handle.'

'Can't we help, Grandy?'

'No, not yet we can't, my boy.'

Dylan knew from past experience that when he got called 'my boy' it was best to leave things alone because whatever the trouble was, it was between adults and nothing to do with him.

'I think I'll take my book outside to read for a while, Grandy.'

'Good idea. I'll do some sorting of my papers.'

Peace was shattered with John's shouting. 'Dylan. Dylan, did you and your friend mess with my things?'

'No, Grandy. Really, we didn't. Liam got a bit cranky when he saw that old photo.'

'Yes, my boy, that's what's missing.'

They each stood watching the other, neither knowing how, or what to say, to diffuse the hostile situation.

Chapter 64

'This would have to be the best BBQ I've been to,' said Ronnie as he looked around at the company he was in. Evans had finally met Jimmy's father and they stood a bit away from the crowd, quietly talking together. Sergeant Brothers was still not totally convinced that Ronnie had nothing to do with the cargo they had captured. Tony Johnson and Billy were chatting like they'd been best mates all their lives. Jimmy began to feel uncomfortable as the only person not involved. He watched Sergeant Brothers flipping the steak while he was still trying to talk with Evans.

'Excuse me, Sarge, but you seem to be a much better talker than a cook, so move over and I'll watch the steaks.'

Now, he felt better. Would he never get rid of this feeling that he didn't belong in either circle, black or white? He supposed not, because of what had happened to his mother. Who, in his eyes, was the most beautiful creature ever created.

'Who's for a steak? They're ready and waiting.'

All the men moved forward with their plates, eagerly waiting to enjoy their meal. The couple of remaining pieces were pushed to the side of the grill so they wouldn't ruin.

'Hey, Jimmy, I've saved a log for you here.'

'Gee, thanks, Ronnie. How the tables have turned. I think I'll really miss your company. It's not every day we have a nice person in our cells.'

'But you don't even know me.'

'Oh, I think I do. My feelings about people are not very often wrong. I know you've got family, tell me about them.'

'Well, let's see. Way back in my youth I met the most exquisite girl that has ever been born. That summer, my dad used to say she was some brown fluff attached to my arm. He meant it in the nicest way, but Leila's parents didn't approve of me at all.'

'Why not, if you were both young and happy?'

'You see, by the end of that summer Leila was expecting a baby, and her father did not want his daughter marrying a white boy. So I had to either disappear and never see Leila or my child, or stand up to him and say we were getting married. All hell broke loose then. The screaming and yelling in their own language, and Leila standing there shaking like a jelly. Her mother dropped a suitcase at our feet, and it was then I realised what was happening. It took Leila a long time before she would tell me exactly what happened that day. The long shot of it is they threw her out with a warning never to come back again.'

Jimmy's eyes were as big as saucers now as he listened to this familiar tale of woe.

'Hey, you two, we're not having a hen's meeting!'

Laughter broke out in their midst, but Jimmy could sense this was a good friendly laughter, not at all like the usual laughter he gets when he's with white friends. He really liked this bloke. Cans were being handed around. Ronnie popped his open and marvelled as to how good it felt to have this cold liquid running down his throat. He then noticed neither Jimmy nor his father had cans. They both were drinking Coke from plastic glasses. He wondered about this but thought better about asking questions when he was having such a good time with these blokes.

Evans was now beside Ronnie. 'Our plane tickets are booked for Wednesday for the three of us.'

'Three! Who else is going?'

'Come on, Ronnie, the injured pilot, of course.'

Now Ronnie's fears came flooding back. Would he really have to go to court and perhaps even bump into Angelo? Evans noticed the genuine shock that registered on Ronnie's face and thought he even saw a slight shudder. It had confirmed Evans' feeling that Ronnie Sims really didn't know what he was getting himself into by being the hired help. He was just a desperate man seeking a quick and easy way of earning a few extra dollars for his large family. Evans also made a mental note not to sit Ronnie anywhere near the pilot, even though it would mean Ronnie would be on his own. Not the best condition for an already scared witness.

The gathering was breaking up. Ronnie wondered where he would sleep as he was no longer a resident guest of the Territory police.

Tony Johnson was walking towards him. 'G'day, Ronnie, we didn't have much time to talk today. How about you spend the night at my place? Billy, Jimmy and his father are staying as well.'

'Geez, mate, that would be great, if it's okay with Brothers.'

'It's all fixed then. I have a couple of jobs to do in town, then I'll come back and pick the three of you up.'

'Right. Yeah, thanks.'

Tony's place was very nice, but Ronnie thought it lacked something. He knew it wasn't the mess or noise that ruled his own home, but there was something missing.

The dwelling was on the outskirts of the town. It was very spacious, five bedrooms plus all the usual rooms of a home.

'Suppose you think this is a bit big for just me to be living in, but the missus was missing the kids since they went away to boarding school, so I told her to go and see them and spend the school holidays with them.'

Tony seemed happy about this arrangement. Ronnie could understand his thinking and where it was coming from. Ronnie tried to think of how he handled being without all the kids.

Chapter 65

J ill Evans could not remember when she last spent an evening out in the company of such a gentleman. Paul Hill was certainly a very special person, and from what Jill had heard around the hospital, a highly respected doctor. The cancellation of her holiday plans had really been a blessing in disguise. If she hadn't gone back to tidy her desk, she may never have run into Dr Paul Hill. Now she was on her own, her mind wandered back to that phone call from Bruce just as they were leaving. He had said he would call because he'd be leaving the Territory soon, as he had a couple of deliveries to make. He'd like to stay with her if her social calendar would allow the time. Tears were forming, but she refused to let them flow. There must have been some reason why he was so short-tempered on the phone. Jill was pacing the floor with her mind in turmoil. How long had she been carrying her personal phone book clutched in her hand? Finally she sat down, and the book fell open onto her lap. She glanced down, and the page was opened at Bruce's former partner in the police force. Now the quandary: should she, should she not? *No, there's been enough mystery*, she thought as her fingers were pushing the numbers. Five, six rings, nobody answered. Jill was about to hang up when a breathless voice sounded in her ear.

'Hello, Detective Alan Carr. Hello, who's there?'

'Oh ... Um ... Alan, it's Jill Evans, Bruce's mother. I was just wondering when you are expecting him?'

'Mrs Evans, how do you know that we are expecting—no, why do you think he's in Australia? He left the force to go to the Middle East with that bunch of do-gooders.'

'Ah ... Well, look, Alan, I'm really sorry, but he's been in the Northern Territory recently, helping with police surveillance in some area up there.'

'Are you sure? Did Bruce ring you? Did he say anything of the nature of his involvement?'

'Well, no, not really. He just asked after a patient that's in the hospital – a child and his mother.'

'Nothing else?'

'No. Is Bruce in some sort of trouble? Alan, please tell me if he is!'

'It's okay, Mrs Evans, really it is. But if he makes contact with you again let me know straight away.'

Jill was now full of apprehension as she placed the phone down. She could make no sense of anything that was going on. *I'm so glad Paul is coming for dinner tonight*, she thought, *because preparing and cooking will keep my mind occupied*

Jill worked feverously during the late afternoon, mentally whipping herself for wasting away the morning on worries. Paul arrived promptly at 7.30pm. Jill was worried still and the tension in the room was thick as fog.

'Jill, would you mind if I make us both a scotch and dry, and we'll just sit and enjoy that lovely CD you've got playing?'

'Oh, look ... I'm sorry, Paul. You must think I have no manners at all, I should have offered.'

'Not at all, my dear, you just seem a little on edge tonight. You haven't had any more phone calls, have you?'

'No. No, not yet, anyway.'

They were now sitting enjoying a drink and each other's company before dinner. Jill was amazed how quickly the tension was disappearing. She thought, *I could get very used to this pampered lifestyle.* Paul was very impressed with the meal. Jill had even made some rum balls to have with their coffee. Whilst they were finishing their coffees, Paul had ventured to place his arm around Jill's shoulder as they sat together on the lounge.

'This is certainly a pleasant evening. It seems a shame that it has to end.'

Jill turned quickly to see Paul stifle a yawn. 'Got an early start with rounds in the morning.'

'Oh … Yes. Yes, Paul.'

Standing at the front door after thanking her again for the wonderful evening. He seemed hesitant to leave but knew he must or he could blow his chances altogether.

'Jill. Jill, dearest, we must do this again.'

'Yes, of course, Paul, any time.'

In a sudden move, he reached over and took Jill into his arms, kissing her gently but passionately. She felt herself give in and even go weak at the knees.

'I really must go.' He was walking towards his car and Jill backed into the doorway, closing the door as his car left the driveway. She stood there hugging herself so she wouldn't loose that wonderful feeling she'd not had for many years. Not since the boys' father had died.

Chapter 66

Marie had no difficulty in finding the room in the library where the meeting was to be held. With her hand on the door, her nerves got the better of her. Marie was just about to step away when a voice behind her said, 'Here, allow me, madam.'

Now Marie had no choice. It was now or never, because the gentleman was holding the door open for her.

'Thank you, thank you very much.'

'You're welcome. I haven't seen you at our meetings before. You are at the right meeting room, aren't you?'

'Oh yes. I've come to try and find some information for a friend. You see, she was born on a Pacific island, although I'm not sure which one.'

Upon entering the room, Marie looked around and was astounded by the number of people. Her heart sank to her feet. How would she ever achieve anything for Leila? She sat in the nearest chair that she could see, wishing the floor would open and swallow her up.

'Ladies and gentlemen, I'd like to open our meeting and to welcome each and everyone here today. As I can see we have a few new faces with us, I think it best that I introduce myself. I am the president and my name is Bobby Tanekaha.'

Marie almost yelled as she heard him – no, it couldn't be, it was just a coincidence. But it certainly got her heart racing. She hadn't noticed how hard she was gripping her bag until the woman in the next seat touched her lightly on the hand and looked inquiringly into Marie's face. Marie could hardly contain herself as they went through the housekeeping parts of the meeting. Did meetings always drag on so long? She glanced at her watch. The meeting had only been going for ten minutes. No, surely not, the watch must have stopped. In her haste she'd not wound it earlier.

The woman who had touched Marie's hand before was now indicating that tea, coffee, and biscuits were being served. Marie's eyes quickly scanned the sea of brown faces and colourful clothing, looking for the one person who could be a key to all the questions. Her fears were mounting until she saw he was still gathering papers together and putting them into a briefcase. Even though Marie's legs felt like jelly, she willed them to at least get her to within speaking distance. She was thinking, *What will I call him? How to ask?*

'Hello. Can I help you again, madam?'

'Oh, I'm sorry, I didn't realise it was you who opened the door.'

'Did you enjoy our discussions? But surely there must be some other reason that brought you to our meeting?'

Marie could feel herself getting hotter and hotter, and the room was beginning to sway at rather odd angles.

'Here, please sit down. I'll get you a drink. I hope I didn't frighten you that much. I don't usually have that effect on ladies.'

Now Marie was feeling more foolish than ever, but she was determined to not let this opportunity get past her, if only for Leila's sake. He sat quietly beside her while she took a few mouthfuls of tea. He was relieved to see the normal colour return to her face.

'Ah ... Mr—'

'No, Bobby. Everyone calls me Bobby, it's easier.'

'Well, yes. I've really come to get some information for someone I've been really friendly with.'

'I see. Does this person have a name?'

'Sorry, yes ... Leila ...'

Now it was Marie's turn to wonder about the wellbeing of the person sitting opposite her.

'Leila, you said?' He even had difficultly saying the name.

'Yes, Leila Sims. I was hoping to make some sort of contact with a family member.'

'But why? Why does this concern you so much?'

'It's a long story, but my grandson and her son have become really good mates. I just believe Liam – that's her son – has a right to know if he has grandparents, too.'

'I see. But, why now? Why start looking now?'

'Well, Leila was very ill recently. In fact, she's still in the hospital. She had twins, but in having them, the doctors found a huge growth that would have killed her, and I suppose when we were talking it came up how much she missed her parents. She is a lovely girl and such a wonderful mother.'

'And what would this wonderful person be requesting if she was to find her family?'

'Nothing. Nothing at all. Well, maybe someone to show off her beautiful babies to.'

'How would they meet? That is if there is such a family. Surely it would be difficult after—how long?'

'Years, ten, maybe eleven years. Maybe someone could go and see the babies, they're the only brown ones in the nursery, and it could progress from there.'

'Do you have an address that this Leila could be contacted at, perhaps a phone number?'

'That's a question I hadn't anticipated. No, I don't, but I could give you mine and I'll gladly pass it on. Or maybe they could ring the hospital before she leaves next week.'

'Tell your friend not to get her hopes up. But who knows what could happen? Maybe a lot, maybe nothing. Now, I have to be going, I've got some matters to take care of.'

'Yes, of course, thanks for your help,' replied Marie as she gathered herself together to leave the room. She turned to have one last look at the helpful man, and saw an elderly gentleman talking to Bobby. *I know that face, but where from?* she thought.

It wasn't until she got on the bus. Marie remembered he'd been the one sitting beside her the day she first went to see Leila and the babies. And hadn't she thought it odd that he caught the lift with her, got out at the maternity ward, then turned around and got straight back in the lift?

Chapter 67

Tony and his visitors had sat around the fireplace in his lounge room until the early hours of the morning. Ronnie found Billy the Beak fascinating, with his stories of struggling with flood and drought on a station that was first owned by his great-grandfather. Ronnie also found it extremely hard to comprehend how a single human being could live so far from regular contact with others. He was thinking how on occasions he'd craved solitary peace and quiet, but would never be able to bear it for months like Billy did. Just at that moment, a face jumped into his mind – Angelo. *Geez, if I hadn't been looking for quiet, I would never have met such a person.* Ronnie broke out in a cold sweat, reliving the threats made before he took on this easy money job. If anything had happened to Leila and the tribe, he knew in his heart he'd never have the courage and willpower to carry on as Billy had. Billy hadn't been sleeping either when he saw Ronnie was awake. Without waking the others, he motioned to Ronnie to come outside.

'Isn't it a bonzer way to start a day? Look over there, Ronnie, now have you ever seen such a sunrise?'

The few clouds that were in the sky were streaked with a crimson glow and the last of the stars were fading away. Nothing stirred; it was as though the two men were the only living souls. Jimmy quietly came outside and saw them. He said nothing to break the spell he knew they were under. He'd seen it happen before to men who'd forgotten to see the beauty of the universe.

'Billy, that was amazing. I've never seen anything like it.'

'Yeah, mate. I didn't figure you to be someone who would have seen the wonder of the morning.'

'It's the spirit of the day taking over from the night spirit,' said Jimmy, startling both the men.

'I suppose you've got a lot of spirit stories locked up inside your head, Jimmy.'

'Yeah, Billy. That is the most precious gift my mother ever gave me. Sometimes I wish she was still here to teach me more.'

Ronnie had been engrossed in watching a blue-tongue lizard stalking about in the leaf fall under the trees.

'Ronnie,' said Jimmy, 'didn't you say your missus knows about the spirits?'

'Yeah, but she doesn't talk about it much anymore. I mean, since her father washed his hands of her when she married me. I know deep down it breaks her heart that there's no contact anymore, but she won't talk about it.'

Billy was listening whilst watching the magic of the morning unfold before his eyes. No matter where he was, he felt it was his duty to welcome each new day.

'Um ... Ronnie ... I know it's none of my business, but the longer your missus and her kin have this wedge between them, the harder it will get to bridge the gap.'

'Yeah, I 'pose, but there's nothing I can do, can I?'

Billy snorted and began to move away before turning back to them.

'I reckon you've never really thought how your missus feels. How would you like to be cut off from the people who raised you to be who you are?'

'Oh … Well, um, I don't suppose I would. But Leila always says it doesn't matter.'

'Is that what her heart says, Ronnie, or only her head?'

'Geez, you two sure know how to make a fella feel like a really low down mongrel.'

'No, Ronnie, I reckon you've just never thought about it from the way your missus sees it.'

Tony had seen the others talking outside, and before joining them, he set about preparing a simple breakfast.

'Chow's up!'

'Hey, Tony, where are you hiding your cook?'

'Now, gents, I'll have none of that. All this was prepared with my own lily-white hands.'

The three visitors were astonished at the meal presented before them.

'No, really, Tony, where's your help?'

'Here, right before you. But if you look in the garbage tin you'll find the wrapper from the bacon slices, shells from the eggs that the hens kindly laid yesterday, and tins that held the baked beans.'

Now they all sat down and hoed into their breakfast. The coffee aroma was too much for Ronnie – he had to ask for a cup, because coffee was his usual breakfast. But as he thought about it, he felt guilty because he only had coffee so he could escape from the unit, Leila, and the kids before the walls began closing in on him. Jimmy excused himself – he said he should ring Sergeant Brothers to find out the plans for the day.

'G'day, Jimmy, thanks for calling. There's nothing doing today. The flight is booked for tomorrow afternoon, so spend the day with your dad.'

As he returned to the others, Billy was saying he really should be getting back to the station to water up the cattle. Tony was having a quiet word to Ronnie.

'Dad, how'd you like to spend the day with yours truly?'

'Hey that'd be great, Jimmy. It's been a while since we had time together.'

Tony looked at Ronnie and nodded his head. 'Okay, Billy, I'll fly you home on one condition: you let Ronnie come and have a look around before he goes off with Detective Evans.'

'Sure ... Sure thing. But the house is a bit of a mess, not like Tony's here.'

'No worries.'

Ronnie was amazed how the people he was meeting lately were so friendly and nice. He really would have to think seriously about getting the housing department to move his family as far away from Angelo as possible.

Chapter 68

Kevin had put himself under an enormous amount of stress just worrying about what should he wear this evening. He'd put on his dark suit, white shirt, and black tie. No, he looked like he was going to a funeral. Next he tried his moleskin trousers with a checked shirt. Now it was pale grey flannel trousers, a pale blue shirt, and navy sports jacket. He held a tie up to the neck of the shirt. No, no tie. At least now he felt he was casual enough, but also dressy. He found he was ready early and, not wanting to sit around, he phoned John and Marie.

'Hello, Marie, it's Kevin.'

'Oh, Kevin, it's nice to hear from you.'

'Marie, could I call on you for an hour? I'm meeting someone and I'm early.'

'Of course There's nothing wrong, is there?'

'No. No, I'll tell you all about it when I get there.'

Puzzled, Marie hung the phone up and wondered what on earth had concerned Kevin.

'John. John, dear, where are you?'

'Right here, woman, trying to see what else our light-fingered house guest took.'

'John.'

'Well, it's true. That old photo from Marsh Flats is gone. You saw how angry Liam got when he saw it. Just hope the little blighter hasn't thrown it away.'

'But surely—'

'But nothing, Marie. I know he took it. Where else could it have got to?'

'I don't know, John. By the way, that was Kevin on the phone, he said he'll drop in shortly.'

'Oh … Your gentleman caller. I'd best disappear for a while.'

Marie was just about to throw her tea towel at John when she saw he was nearly bursting from trying not to laugh.

'What's he coming for?'

'Don't know, just asked if he could drop by.'

They didn't have to wonder for too long because the squeaky gate announced his arrival.

'Wow, now I know you're after my wife.'

Kevin spluttered. 'Excuse me?'

'Oh, don't mind him, Kevin, but you do look very handsome this evening. Anything we should know about?'

'Well, yes and no.'

'Okay, Kevin, you've got my attention,' John butted in.

Marie was getting very cross with the way John was always baiting Kevin. He knew how nervous Kevin was.

'Well, I'm going out tonight—'

'Not with my wife you're not.'

Marie took hold of Kevin's arm and headed towards the living room in the front of the house.

'Hello,' said Dylan, looking up from a game he was playing on the television screen.

'Hi, Dylan. Who's winning?'

'Not me, that's for sure.'

'Kevin, please, don't take any notice of John. Sometimes he just doesn't know when to be serious.'

'It's okay, Marie. I feel rather honoured that he feels he should protect your safety when I'm around.'

'Oh, Kevin, stop it, you're getting just as bad.'

Dylan looked up again, and watched as his Nana and this nice looking man were pretending to be angry with each other. He thought, *Adults are really not that much different from kids, only bigger.*

'I'm taking Barbara out for dinner tonight and I was hoping for your verdict on my choice of clothes.'

'You look fine, Kevin, but you don't need my approval. Barbara must have decided you were okay in whatever clothes you had on when you asked her out.'

'Do you really think so?'

'Yes, of course. I'd be glad if I was Barbara tonight.'

Now Kevin was blushing and Marie kicked herself for being so outspoken. Dylan diffused it by saying, 'I think it's great you didn't wear a tie.'

'I thought I should see if there are any questions about Marsh Flats that I might talk about, or whether I should just leave that subject completely alone.'

'Oh, dear … Here I was thinking you came just to see me, well I never.'

Before Kevin had time to answer, she'd left the room to collect John.

Dylan now turned around to face the visitor. 'Is this your first time out with this girl? I don't really think Grandy can give you any advice on girls. You see he's only been out with Nana. It must have been a hundred years ago when he first asked her out.'

'Hey! I heard that Dylan. I'll have you know I'm not that old, nor am I out of practice.'

'Yeah. Sorry, Grandy. I didn't mean anything.'

'Kevin, come out with me into the men's domain. Now, as for Marsh Flats tonight, don't you bring it up, just talk about your family and see where it ends up, okay?'

'Thanks, John. I'll let you know if I learn anything I think is important.'

'Good man, Kevin. Have a great time.'

Kevin left the Hunter household in high spirits. He was thinking about Barbara when he almost ran a red light. *Oh well, it was the colour red that first caught my attention. Boy, I hope everything goes well tonight.*

Chapter 69

Di Brown had been in the house checking that things were in order. She could hardly contain her pleasure at the thought of her childhood home once again being filled with children's laughter. *I do hope Leila will allow me to help sometimes, perhaps sit with the babies while she has a nap,* thought Di. The one problem that so far she had not been able to fix was the whereabouts of Mr Sims, and whether he would approve of the plans made in his absence. How was it possible for him to literally drop off the face of the earth, leaving not even a slight inkling of where he'd gone? Di had been absolutely astounded by the way Leila was so calm about her husband and the immense faith she had that he would just turn up when his job had been finished. Until she realised that she'd seen the look in Leila's eyes that could only register as the look of pure love.

'I will have to ring Angie, see if she knows anything more,' Di said to herself, as she locked the house up for maybe the last time. Walking down towards her unit, Di could hear her answering machine talking to a caller. 'Mrs Brown, please come into the welfare office at your earliest convenience. We have heard of Mr Sims' location.'

Now Di began to worry. Did the voice sound ominous, or was it her imagination? If only she didn't have to wait until tomorrow. Why did they call so late in the day with a message like that? She had to ring Angie and tell her the news.

'Hello, Angie. Yes, it's Di Brown. Any chance you could meet me for coffee this evening? My shout, of course, this time.'

'Well, how can a person turn down an invitation like that? I will meet you at 7.30, okay?'

'Yes, thanks, Angie. Bye now, it sounds like you've got your hands full at the moment.'

Meanwhile, back at the Sims', Angie was doing the juggling act of trying to manage all of the Sims' kids.

'Helen, I'll help you bath the kids if Barbara will feed the little ones.'

'Sure, Angie. Got a hot date, have we?'

'No. It was Di Brown, she sounded quite worried. I'm meeting her for coffee at 7.30. I do hope it's nothing too serious, because we've come too close to getting this family a second chance at a normal life.'

'Sorry, Angie. Yes, you go by all means. Like you, we hope it's nothing serious.'

Angie left Barbara and Helen with the kids and quickly hurried out the door to ensure she made it to the café in time for her meeting with Di.

Angie's face dropped as she saw Di coming through the café door. She waved to her friend to indicate she'd got a table in a quiet corner of the room.

'Whatever has gone wrong Di? We're all geared up ready for the move on Wednesday.'

'Yes, I know. The department left a message on my phone. It was too late for me to ring this afternoon, but I've got to see them tomorrow. It's something to do with Mr Sims' whereabouts.'

'Excuse me, ladies, I'm not in the habit of eavesdropping, but I heard you've lost a Mr Sims.'

Two shocked faces were now staring at the stranger who had admitted to eavesdropping on their conversation. 'Oh, look, I'm Doctor Paul Hill. I work at the hospital where Leila and Liam are patients. I'm also a good friend of a nurse there, Jill Evans.'

'If you don't mind, we were having a private conversation.'

'Yes, I know, it's very rude of me, but Mr Sims is arriving here sometime Wednesday or Thursday.'

'How do you know that?'

'It's a long story. If I may be permitted to join you both, I'll try and fill you in.'

Both Di and Angie were still in shock, but they managed a brief bow to the doctor, who then proceeded to sit down at their table and start talking.

'My friend Jill has a son who was in the police force and at the moment he's with Mr Sims in the Northern Territory, somehow helping with police investigations. I'm sorry, I'm still a little vague on the details, but it does seem that Mr Sims has earned a great deal of respect from the police up there. Something to do with plugging a leak.'

Paul shrugged his shoulders at this last remark to indicate that he had no idea what it meant either.

'Look, I'm sorry if I've ruined your evening coffee, but it was too much of a coincidence to hear his name again,' Paul said as he rose and put his chair back at the other table.

'Well, I never, Angie, what are we involved in?'

'I'm sure it will all work out properly in the end, Di.'

'Oh, I hope so. But what do I say or do tomorrow with the department?'

'Yes. I think I'd let them tell you everything as though you have heard nothing of that story tonight.'

'Angie, we are doing the right thing, aren't we? It never occurred to me that there would be as many problems as we've had with this family. All I saw at the beginning was a way of helping Liam and his family to have a better living environment. It wasn't selfish to also be getting some live-in company as well, was it?'

'No, Di, of course not, don't even think that. By the way, did you see Leila on the weekend?'

'Yes, and as she looked at the photos, she was reduced to tears of happiness. She also came to her own conclusion that I was the guardian the department had mentioned to her.'

'How did she take that news?'

'Once again, she was overwhelmed with gratitude. I really don't think anything can go wrong now, we're so close.'

Angie now turned to face Di and, while trying not to laugh, asked if this coffee evening was going to be completely without coffee. Their corner of the cafe was now filled with laughter, which also brought the waitress, who until now had not approached their table.

Chapter 70

Marie was bursting with excitement when she arrived home from the meeting at the library. As she opened the front door she called, 'John, John. You won't believe how well the meeting went.'

Then her bubble burst: she was talking to herself in an empty house. Of course, Dylan's treatment – how could she have possibly forgotten that was where Dylan and John were now? Marie began thinking how she would love to rush to the hospital right now and tell Leila about how kind the people were, and how the president of the group promised to do what he could, but he didn't want her to get her hopes up. Marie was in the bedroom getting changed when the tell-tale gate let her know John was arriving home. She rushed, still pulling her arms into the old but comfortable jumper. 'John. John, you'll never guess.'

'What, my dear? That it's fashionable to wear jumpers inside out now?'

'What?'

'Your jumper – the seams are on the outside.'

Marie couldn't decide whether to remove the item or just leave it, seeing as it was already on, and she wasn't going anywhere. It stayed on as it was.

'You'll never guess what I've learnt from the meeting.'

'No, Marie. I'll pop the kettle on so you can relax and gather your thoughts while I make us a cuppa.'

'Thanks, John. I nearly didn't go in, but as I was backing away from the door I bumped into a man who turned out to be the president of the group. And even more amazing, his surname is the same as Leila's.'

'Here, Marie, have your tea. Do you want anything to go with it?'

'No thanks. John, where's Dylan?'

'I was wondering when you'd notice his absence.'

'But, where is he?'

'Visiting with Liam. I said we'd pick him up in a couple of hours.'

As the phone began ringing, Marie picked it up, and for a moment, John thought she'd got some sort of electric shock with the way she dropped the phone. John bent down to pick it up but Marie beat him to it.

'Could you please say that again?' Marie asked, her heart beating fast.

'Yes, Mrs Hunter. I would like to meet you in the foyer of the hospital where Mrs Sims is a patient,' said Bobby Tanekaha, the president of the meeting that Marie had attended just a few hours ago this morning.

'Really? I mean, we only spoke a few hours ago. You said probably nothing would come of my enquiries.'

'Sometimes people can be lucky.'

'Will you be alone? My husband will be coming because our grandson is visiting with Liam.'

'No, I will not be alone. I'll have a couple of elderly people with me, but please don't jump to any wrong conclusions, it may not work out.'

'Of course not, what time shall we meet?'

'How about an hour from now?'

'Yes. Yes, and thank you.'

John could see how much of a turmoil his wife's brain was in by the way she had sat down in the chair and stared vacantly into space.

'John. John, dear, we have to go to the hospital. I need to meet with someone.'

'You mean, something has already come up through your meeting at the library?'

'Yes, John, isn't it wonderful?'

'It is, but please tread carefully. I don't want you to get hurt.'

Without another thought, Marie hurried to the bedroom to put her better clothes on again. She began thinking, *I do hope it is good news. What will I have to say to them? No, I'll let Bobby do the talking, because he's the one that's making this possible.*

'Marie, you ready yet, or do I have to go to the hospital by myself? You've been changing for the past half an hour.'

This brought Marie back to the present, instead of being off in the land of promise.

'Sorry, John, yes, I'm ready.'

Parking was terrible so John let Marie out near the main entrance before going to find a parking spot. He'd hardly left when a car pulled out quite near, so he was back in time to see a wonderful experience happening before his eyes in the foyer.

Chapter 71

J ill was having the most pleasant dream when it was interrupted by the phone ringing.

'Hello?'

'Oh, look, I'm sorry I've woken you up. I forgot about the time difference. It's just I thought I'd call you, Mum, before going to bed, because I'm flying down your way tomorrow.'

'Bruce. Bruce, it is you.'

'Well, I hope you don't have other phone calls from men at this hour.'

'Are you really coming? I think I did something you won't like – I rang Alan Carr.'

'You what? Why on earth did you do that?'

'Well, I thought you were in a lot of trouble and wouldn't tell me.'

'Oh, Mum, I'm a big boy now. You don't have to look out for my welfare.'

'Can I meet you at the airport?'

'No, sorry, you can't. I'll explain it all to you when I get home. Perhaps I'll take you out for dinner.'

'Yes. Yes, that'd be nice. Please be careful at whatever you're doing.'

'Oh, um ... I suppose I should meet your Doctor Hill and apologise for my behaviour. It was just a shock to realise that my own mother would be going out on a date.'

'Yes. Thank you, I think, Bruce. Now, I need to get some sleep if you're coming home again.'

As Bruce put the phone back in its cradle, he sat back in the chair and began to realise how much unwanted pressure and worry he'd caused his mother. The job he'd been on was undercover and extremely dangerous. If he'd had any idea of the details, he probably would have turned it down. But then, he'd achieved a great result, captured all the cargo in Australia, netted a lot of small players, whilst his offsider in the Middle East had caught most of the king pins. In fact, the force had managed all this without much involvement from Ronnie, just his help with a couple of names, so as far as Bruce was concerned, he was free to go back to his family after a few formalities were tidied up. As for himself, he would not be in the undercover drug scene again – he'd got to know too many people in the Middle East and he was really looking forward to shaving this annoying beard off, and returning to his natural colour and hair style. Perhaps they'd find him a really nice comfortable desk where he'd write up the information he'd gathered during the past couple of years.

Morning broke through and for some reason Bruce had an uneasy feeling. He went round to the station to have breakfast with Brothers.

'G'day, mate. Look, I don't know if I did the right thing earlier with a phone call from down south. I said I'd never heard of you.'

'Oh. Do you know who the caller was and what was wanted?'

'I believe so. With this bust you've just completed, were there any other southern cops involved besides the ones you've contacted?'

'No, why?'

'Well, this Detective Alan Carr was on the phone early, I mean real early, this morning. Luckily the phone was diverted to me at home.'

'I see.' Bruce's mind was whirling flat-out. 'Maybe my mum's phone call opened the missing link.'

'What are you on about, Evans?'

'Well, last night I rang my mum to tell her I'd be home soon. She told me she'd rung Alan Carr out of concern for my welfare. I got mad and told her she should not have done that, but now maybe I'll have to thank her.'

'Brothers, I need to delay breakfast 'til I've got in touch with my super. I think he'll be very interested to have a little chat with Detective Carr. I would never have believed he was a bent cop, but thinking back, he always seemed to manage on his wage, while I was usually scraping by the day before payday. He was my partner and I couldn't see what he was up to, so how would anyone else? But his head will roll with all the others,' said Bruce.

A while later they were walking back from the café after devouring two very large breakfasts.

'You know, Evans, I think I'm going to miss having your ugly face around here, and I know Jimmy's going to miss our guest.'

Chapter 72

Barbara had been dithering all day. Yes she was excited about going out with Kevin. If only the orphanage had chosen a better day to send her a file – they'd found it when the builder was doing the renovations. She just wanted to sit down quietly and digest the information. To sit down quietly with the Sims tribe ... now that would be a miracle. Suzy had been in a terrible humour all day, none of the others could get anywhere near her without her screaming. In fact, Mr Black had come and knocked on the door to make sure everything was alright. No, she must put it down and think about it tomorrow. She was going to enjoy the night out with Kevin. Barbara was still carrying the dilapidated looking file in her hand as she went to answer the door, thinking it was Mr Black again.

'Hello, Barbara. I know I'm a bit early, but I couldn't wait to see you again.' Seeing no reaction on her face, he asked, 'I can wait in the car, if you like? You do still want to go out this evening, don't you?'

'What? Yes, of course. Oh, look, I'm sorry, Kevin, I was a million miles away then.'

'Yes, I saw that. Look, if you want to leave it to some other night, I understand.'

'No, Kevin, I've been waiting all day to see you too, but of all days, I received this in the mail.' Barbara held it out for him to see – it was an old file about her partly unknown childhood from the orphanage she'd told him about.

'This has upset you? I thought you said they'd lost your file. Now you can find answers to all your questions.'

Barbara burst into tears. Without thinking, Kevin pulled her towards him and stepped out of the doorway, closing the door and leading her towards the stairs. He kept his arm around her shoulders as her head lay on his chest. Gradually, her sobbing eased and, like in films he'd seen, Kevin flicked open a clean white handkerchief, which she took and began mopping up the tears.

'Kevin, I'm so sorry. I wasn't even going to mention getting this silly old piece of junk.'

'No, I think if you'd like, we should take your junk to dinner with us. You know, two heads are better than one and all that nonsense. What do you say, Barbara?'

'Oh, Kevin.' Her bottom lip began to quiver.

'Think nothing of it. I mean, one day when you're the mother of my children, I would like to know that you don't have any unmentionable skeletons tucked away.'

'Kevin, what you just said, did you mean ... Or are you just trying to pacify me?'

'No, Barbara, I meant it. But let's just take it slowly, I don't want to ruin my chances by rushing.'

With that, she left him with the file while she went back into the unit to patch up her face and hair.

Suzy came rushing up to her. 'Did he 'urt ya?'

'No, Suzy. I was just a little sad.'

'Mmm ... I don't fink we'll be sad tomorrow!'

She was walking back to join her brother's game and Barbara was too stunned to ask Suzy what she meant. Leaving the bathroom feeling a little more human, she went to find Angie to let her know she was going out a little earlier.

'Angie, has Suzy been talking to you today?'

'Yes, but a lot I didn't understand.'

'She just told me she won't be sad tomorrow.'

'I know, it's as though she knows what's going to happen. In fact, it tends to get a bit spooky,' said Angie. 'Bye, Barbara. Have a great evening.'

'Thanks, I will.'

As Angie turned around, Suzy was standing so near they both nearly toppled over.

'What's wrong, Suzy?'

'Nuffin', Angie. We're goin' somewhere nice tomorrow an' me dad's coming 'ome.'

'Really? How do you know that?'

'Just know.'

'What if things don't happen the way you think they will?'

'It will, Angie,' she called over her shoulder whilst making her way to the bedroom.

Angie began thinking about how wonderful it was going to be to sleep in a proper bed, not just on an inflatable mattress or sometimes the sofa. She was really going to miss this little family, but it would be nice to have a life of her own again. Perhaps she might even see more of Tim Cook. How was Di Brown going to handle the change from complete peace to non-stop childhood noise? But then, being a teacher for all those years, she was probably used to it by now.

'Angie, what's for tea? We're 'ungry.'

Where had those last few hours gone? *No panic, it's all prepared, all I have to do is heat it up. Helen should be here by then so it won't be a feeding frenzy at the zoo.*

'I'm just heating it up now. Won't be long at all. Have you washed your face and hands? Suzy, please help the little ones.'

Suzy grunted. 'I'm glad Mam's comin' 'ome.'

Now that really did start a frenzy.

'Thanks, Suzy, thanks a lot. Now, explain it's only a feeling you have. You don't really know when she will be coming home.'

'But she is,' wailed Suzy, who in turn set off the little ones as well.

Angie was silently praying, *Please, God, get me through this night and somehow make Suzy's predictions come true.*

Chapter 73

Marie entered the hospital and three sets of eyes fastened their focus on her. She stood quite still gathering her emotions together until they were under control. Bobby came towards her, leaving the other two behind. He held out his hand, thanking Marie for coming as he shook her hand.

'Do you have any idea what you have started by coming to that meeting and asking questions for your friend?'

'No, I don't, but I meant no harm to anyone.'

'If you don't mind, I'd like to meet your friend before the other two. We don't want to upset anyone unnecessarily, do we?'

'Of course not. Maybe they could wait in the kiosk.'

'Yes, I'll tell them that. Then we'll go.'

It was very uncomfortable in the elevator. Marie was glad when they all got out.

'Should I go and see Leila first? I mean, to let her know she's got a visitor?'

'No. We will go in together, then you can witness firsthand the outcome of what you started.'

Now Marie was feeling terrible. Whatever did he mean? But there was no backing out now, because they were outside Leila's door. Marie gently knocked and they entered together. Leila's face became frozen in shock. Marie couldn't decide whether it was happiness or fear. Then it all happened too quickly. Bobby rushed towards the bed, as Leila put her arms out.

'Oh Bobby, Bobby, I've missed you all so much. Marie, dear Marie, I didn't hold any hope for you finding any of my family, but you did it so quickly!'

'Mrs Hunter, please stay with my sister whilst I go and get something from the kiosk for her.'

'You don't have to, Bobby. Please stay so I can look at you.'

'Have you forgotten that a family member always brings a gift when visiting another? I promise I won't spend a lot and I won't be long.'

With those parting words, Marie understood she wasn't to say anything about the gift, and she also realised that the couple were Leila's parents. Bobby had wanted to make sure of Leila's identity before exposing them.

'How did you do it, Marie? How did you know where to start?'

'Leila, it was almost a meeting of pure chance. You see, I bumped into Bobby as I was chickening out of going to the meeting. I take it he is really your brother?'

'Yes, Marie. He is, and I haven't seen him since he was fourteen years old.'

The two women turned towards the door as it opened slowly. Bobby came in carrying a small bunch of flowers. He caught the deflated look on Marie's face, but then watched both their faces as he ushered his parents into the room.

'Princess, my princess. I didn't know if I would live to see the day when my princess would see her father again.'

'Oh, Papa. I've missed you and Mama so much. If it hadn't been for my friend here, it would not have become possible. I thought you never wanted to see me ever again.'

'I know I said those words when I was very upset, but I never dreamt we would be parted for all these years.'

The tension was growing in the room. Marie felt as though she was intruding on this very private family gathering.

'Excuse me, Leila, do you think it would be a good time for Liam to visit? After all, it was because he thought he didn't have any grandparents that this hunt started.'

Just at that moment, a nurse popped her head around the door. 'Just checking,' she said.

'Ah, nurse. Do you think someone could bring Liam up to see his mum?'

'Yes, I'll organise it straight away.'

Dylan and Liam were chattering away while John continued reading his paper.

'Mr Hunter, would you and Dylan mind escorting Liam up to his mum's room? She requires his presence, if he's not too busy, that is.'

'What's wrong with Mam?'

'Nothing, Liam, she just wants to see you, and as Dylan's grandmother is there, you might as well all go, okay?'

'Come on, Mr Hunter, push faster.'

'That's a bit unfair, how will Dylan keep up?'

Now he slunk back into his chair and was quiet the rest of the trip. A nurse was waiting for them.

'I'll let your mother know you're here. Just wait a moment.'

The door opened and Liam was amazed to see the multitude of faces in his mother's room. There was no way his brain could work out what on earth was going on. His eyes stopped on the face of the older man – he'd seen him before. He was the one who'd been up there looking at his babies. But why was he here with his mam?

'Mam, what's wrong? Why are they 'ere? That one's been lookin' at the twins.' He accused with the pointing of his finger.

'Liam, dear, come closer. You know how much you envy Dylan's grandparents? Well, now you've got some yourself.'

'Wha'd'ya mean?' He felt he had to act tough because his world was changing too fast for his mind to understand the implications of what his mother had just said.

'Hey, Liam, that's great. Now when I talk about Nana and Grandy you won't have to get mad.'

'Yeah, well …'

Bobby had taken his chair towards where his own parents stood.

'Liam, these people are your mother's parents.'

'But … I thought Mam said—'

'It's a very, very long story, but now it will have a happy ending, because we have finally met you. We're looking forward to meeting your father and your brothers and sisters as well.'

Leila flashed a quick look towards her father, but the look on his face said it was okay, and all was forgiven. All she needed was to somehow find Ronnie before all the happiness blew up in her face. She offered a quick request to whichever spirits were listening. *Please bring Ronnie home to us quickly.* Conversation was filling the room – everyone seemed to be completely at ease. Leila was wishing she had tried harder to contact her parents, but nothing mattered now as she finally had them.

A nurse came into the room and had to speak loudly to be heard over the noise.

'Quiet, please, party time is over. Patients back to bed, and visitors say your goodbyes. Thank you.'

Marie and John started towards the door. Dylan was a little reluctant until Liam asked John to push his chair.

'Ya know what Dilly, this will be the last time anyone pushes me around 'cause me and Mam are goin' 'ome tomorrow.'

Marie sighed loudly, causing Dylan to ask, 'Nana, you alright, are you Nana?'

'Yes, dear, it's just—what's that old saying, John? Oh, I remember, "God's in his heaven and all is right with the world." I just feel I've experienced the most wondrous day of my life.'

All three males looked at Marie and then they shook their heads while John muttered, 'Women, what strange creatures they are, but I couldn't live without mine.'

Chapter 74

J immy's father was at the airport to supervise the loading of what was thought to be items of his departed wife. None of the staff thought anything was unusual, because they knew how much he still loved her. When he'd finished, he called Brothers. Now the wheels were in motion. Evans had spent the past half an hour at the hospital getting the history on the patient he was taking down south. The noise of an unscheduled small plane worried Brothers and Evans so much that they raced together to the airport. As it was descending, the sun was stopping a clear view, and it wasn't until it taxied to a halt that Brothers could see it was Tony Johnson. What surprised them more was the fact that Billy was there as well as Ronnie.

'You're cutting it fine, mate.'

'Yeah, I know, but your guest couldn't get enough of the views, could ya mate?'

'No, it was amazing.'

'What are you doing here, Billy?'

'I'm having a holiday. I'm spending a week or so with Tony.'

'But what about your stock? They've never managed without you before.'

'That's why we were a bit late. We filled every bore trough and opened most of the gates, so they should be okay. If not, it's the bank's loss, not mine.'

Sergeant Brothers registered a little concern on his face but thought it was better not to interfere in another man's doings.

'Yeah, right! You know what you're doing.'

'Sure do. In fact, I might even hunt down the missus. The company I've had recently showed me how much I really miss her and the kids. I know she'd never come back to live on the station, but maybe if she lived here in town I could occasionally see her. Who knows.'

This got Ronnie thinking about what he would return to. Maybe Evans would let him try once more to phone the unit. He just wanted to hear the noise of his kids. *Hear the noise*, he thought. Wasn't it the noise that he was escaping from that got him involved with Angelo in the first place? Even thinking the name made a cold shiver run down his spine.

'You okay, Ronnie? I know it's early morning, but I wouldn't have thought the temperature was cool enough to make you shiver.'

'No, I'm fine, really. Are we going to the police office before it's time to leave?'

Brothers and Evans both turned with worried looks.

'Why do you ask? You haven't left anything behind.'

'No, I know. I was just hoping to use the phone one more time. You know, to try and get an answer from the unit. Are you sure he hasn't got me kids?'

'Look, it's okay, mate,' Evans said, trying to reassure Ronnie.

'The boys down there already have your friend Angelo and some of his friends snugly locked up behind bars. He was silly enough to be carrying a small amount when he was picked up for routine questioning.'

'Look, he's no friend.'

'Take it easy.'

'When you say picked up, you mean he won't make the connection to me?'

'It's all taken care of. You never made it to the drop off.'

'How about I ask the boys to go to your unit, and if we're lucky they'll radio us back before the plane is ready to leave.'

It didn't sound real good, but it was the only choice he had. After nodding his head, Evans went back to the police car and put wheels in motion to try and relieve Ronnie's agony of not knowing what was happening to his family.

'Hey, Ronnie, come back over here for a second.'

Ronnie looked towards the darkened hanger. With the contrasts of dark and light, he couldn't even see the person, but he recognised Jimmy's voice.

'Yeah, mate, what is it?'

'They're just bringing the patient from the hospital. He's first to go on board and he'll be last off.'

'Hey, but he'll see me and he'll talk to Angelo. Oh, hell, why didn't Evans think about him seeing me?'

'But he has. You see, our friend is occupying the last seat at the back with Detective Evans. He'll be cuffed to the seat, window shade down, and a screen between him and the other passengers.'

'Oh. Well, that makes me feel a bit easier about travelling in the same plane.'

Bruce Evans had put the request through for Ronnie and so far nothing. Time was beginning to run out. *Poor devil,* he thought. *It must be eating him alive not knowing.*

Evans finished helping Jimmy secure both their captive passenger and the merchandise. Brothers was waving his arms, Evans hurried over.

'Sorry, mate. That was the south boys. Looks like the unit's been cleared out, there's not a soul there. Also, listen to this: Mrs Sims, her son, and the babies are no longer in the hospital.'

'Hell and damnation, what's happened? If I find Alan Carr had anything to do with this, I think I'll personally do him in myself.' He began pacing up and down thumping one fist into the other. 'I've got to make one quick phone call before Ronnie and I board the plane. Hopefully my mum will know what's going on with the Sims family.'

He spoke a mite too abrasive to start with before his mother pulled him up short. Yes, she knew all about Mrs Sims. It was the most wondrous event that was happening today. After listening to all the details, he had just one request.

'Could you and your doctor friend come to the airport to meet the plane and bring Mrs Sims with you?'

'He's not my doctor friend, Bruce. He's Paul Hill, and I'm very fond of him, and I was hoping you would like him too.'

'Yeah, yeah, Mum. Look, I've got to go, the plane's waiting for me.'

'Okay, Bruce, we'll see you when you arrive.'

Chapter 75

The welfare department, for some reason, were being extremely nice to the Sims family. Neither Angie, Helen, nor Barbara could ever remember the department sending a removalist van complete with crew. They even sent a set-up mini bus for the children with instructions they were all to go to the hospital to collect Liam, his mum, and the new babies.

Helen and Barbara were organising the children. Mr Black came out to say goodbye and gave Helen a bag of lollies to be shared out later. Angie watched as the last of the meagre amount of belongings were placed in boxes.

Oh, she thought. *That's why we haven't had any phone calls lately.* The telephone plug was partly pulled out of its socket on the wall. It hadn't been noticed because an armchair had always sat in front of it.

Angie pulled the door shut for the last time. Mr Black came over and took her hand. 'You really got some gift wiv them kids. I didn't think it possible for anyone to control 'em. Where they goin', miss?'

'Sorry, Mr Black, you know how the department works, but I'll tell you what I think. When they are all settled, I'll ask Leila to get in touch. But she'll be very busy for the next couple of months, you know, with the new twins and trying to settle into somewhere new.'

'You know, miss, that Suzy's a strange one. She told me the other day somethin' was goin' to 'appen today, but she said her dad were coming 'ome too. He hasn't, has he?'

'No, Mr Black, he hasn't. I'm sorry, but I really must be going. It's taken a lot longer to get organised and I still need to take the children to the hospital. Doctor Hill asked especially for them all to come and collect Leila and Liam, heaven only knows why. I would have thought Leila might enjoy her last little bit of peace and quiet.'

'You know, miss, I fink Leila enjoys the kid noise.'

Angie waved goodbye as she headed down to where Helen and Barbara were waiting with the kids.

'Okay, who threatened whom and with what?'

'Don't look at us, Angie. It was something Suzy said to them. Whatever it was has turned them into complete angels.'

The three women were buckling and strapping their little charges in for possibly the last time. Suzy had arranged which seats were to be left for her mum and Liam. Once again, she became adamant that the front seat was to be left for her father.

The little bus pulled into the hospital. Liam was really anxious to talk with his brothers and sisters. Two nurses brought the twins out and put them into their capsules. Angie wondered why Doctor Hill and Sister Evans were walking one each side of Leila, but now they too were getting on the bus. Once again, Suzy had it all organised. The bus pulled away and re-entered the traffic, but it was going in the wrong direction.

'Excuse me, I think we're going the wrong way, driver.'

Doctor Hill assured them it was okay, they just had a small detail to attend to on the way. Angie could see Suzy hugging herself as if she had to hold in whatever she knew that everyone else didn't.

'Doctor Hill, we're heading for the airport. Why?'

'Sorry, can't say. I'm just following orders.'

As the bus was approaching the entrance, it suddenly took another route towards the cargo receivable depot. This was really beginning to unnerve Angie.

'Won't be long, we just have to back up here and pick up two items of cargo.'

Suzy was now out of her seat and heading towards the front of the bus.

'Suzy. Suzy, please, sit down.'

'But I want to see 'im. I do, I do.'

Now it was Leila's turn to start beaming – her face had become radiant. *What is it with this family,* thought Angie as she turned and shrugged her shoulders towards Barbara and Helen. A scream caused her to swing back so fast she cracked her neck.

'Da, Da, I knew you were coming,' said Suzy as Mr Sims and Bruce Evans entered the bus.

'Gee, I was hoping for that sort of welcome, but I'll settle for a hug, Mum, and then I'd like to know who this handsome hunk is sitting beside you,' Bruce said to his mum, Jill.

Jill turned bright red as she told Bruce that she didn't think he'd ever grow up. The driver started the engine and informed his passengers he wouldn't stop again until they had reached their destination. Ronnie wondered what he'd meant by this, but was too content in the midst of his family to even care.

Chapter 76

'Nana, could we please go and visit Liam? He said he's leaving this week.'

'I know, darling, but no, you can't. He's already left with his mum.'

'Why did Liam think he didn't have any grandparents when he really did, Nana?'

'It's hard to explain. Maybe after we've finished lunch, Grandy will help me explain it to you.'

'Conspiring again, are you, boy? What am I going to explain?'

'About Liam and his grandparents.'

John began putting a few papers on the kitchen table.

'Oh, no you don't. I said after lunch not now.'

The squeak from the gate alerted them to expect a guest or two. Both Marie and John were surprised to see Kevin, but more surprised that he had a young lady with him. Eyes flashed their secret messages between John and Marie.

'Sorry to intrude without phoning first, but we have brought something to share with you. I mean food and information!'

'And who is this ravishing beauty, Kevin?'

It was too hard to tell who was blushing the most.

'I'm sorry,' stammered Kevin. 'This is Barbara. Barbara, this is John and Marie Hunter and their grandson Dylan.'

'Pleased to meet you. Kevin said you have an interest in Marsh Flats and people who live or lived there. I have just received a whole file of information that was discovered by accident when the orphanage where I once lived was being refurbished.'

John's eyes were shining like lanterns and Marie was sure she could even see him quivering.

'We were just thinking about lunch, so we'll leave all the information until later please, John.'

'Oh, drat, woman.'

'Grandy, you shouldn't say that to Nana.'

'Thank you, Dylan. Now, I'll set the table.'

'May I help, Marie?' asked Barbara, as she placed a barbeque chicken on the bench.

'Perhaps you could tear up the lettuce while I check the potato salad, tomatoes and cucumbers.'

When the chicken and salad lunch was finished, John was a little too eager to be done with eating. As he began easing himself away from the table, Marie produced the dessert.

'Couldn't we have this later, Marie, perhaps tonight?'

'John ...'

He could now see the trap he'd blundered into. How could a host produce a dessert only to take it away again, because they wanted the meal done with and finished?

'Look, Kevin, old boy. I'm sorry I let my manners slip away, but it's only because of your friend's papers. They may just be the missing link I've been looking for for years.'

'Don't worry, John. Barbara and I are not going anywhere.'

Chapter 77

Ronnie was relaxing in the noise of this little bus, but he was thinking, *No, it's not noise, it's kids interacting*. The bus was certainly taking a roundabout way of getting them all home, but he did like the look of the suburb they were going through now – such wide streets with those big, leafy trees growing along each side of the footpath. The houses were big rambling styles set well back from the street with beautiful gardens. Ronnie was totally at ease with Suzy curled up on his lap, but why was the driver slowing now? Then he saw the police.

'Hell.' He swung around to face Bruce Evans with such fury in his face. 'I thought you said if I helped you, you'd help me. Well, thanks very much, mate.'

Bruce had not asked for or even thought that the police would turn up. Once again, his first thought was Alan Carr.

'Look, Ronnie, if it's any consolation, that cop's news to me too. I certainly didn't ask for them.'

'Yeah, but they're here now, and he'll put the cuffs on me in front of the kids.'

Angie was now catching snippets of the angry conversation between Leila's husband and the other man. Then she saw Tim and realised he was in uniform. He would not have even thought to change clothes because the kids had seen him as a policeman. Somehow, she had to diffuse the situation before it got any worse. Barbara did it for her as she turned around to Angie.

'My, my, isn't that your officer, Tim Cook? He turns up wherever you go.'

It was Bruce Evans' turn now to be on the wrong end of the conversation. 'You mean he's a friend of yours?'

'Not only mine, but the children's as well. In fact, it's through a lot of his hard work that everything has finally come together today.'

There were some very puzzled faces among the adult passengers. Now, the driver had stopped the engine of the bus. It was Suzy who saw her first.

'There's Mrs Brown. Why is she waving? How did she know we're on the bus, Liam?'

'I dunno, Suzy, but I'm not goin' to school today.'

'No, silly, it's still holidays.'

'Oh, yeah. I knew that.'

As the driver had turned the engine off, he opened the door.

Mrs Brown stepped aboard as he was shutting it again, before his young passengers could escape. Bruce Evans was making his way between bodies to where Ronnie was sitting.

'Hope you can throw some light on whatever is going on here. I was only to see you safely home without running into any unwanted friends,' said Bruce.

'Beats me, mate. I don't know what's happening,' replied Ronnie.

Mrs Brown, in her skilled teacher manner, soon had everyone sitting very quietly. She didn't go into a lot of detail, but the gist of it was she wanted Ronnie and Leila to follow her, whilst the others looked after the children.

Ronnie was more puzzled than ever, but as he looked at his wife, he saw she had that serenity about her that she'd had way back in the first summer they spent together. They followed, arm in arm, down the short pathway to the front door of the house. Di Brown opened the door and asked them inside.

'Look, Mrs Brown, if it's about the kids behaviour at school, couldn't it wait a couple of days? I've only just come home and I haven't even held my new babies.'

'Shh … Ronnie, Mrs Brown—ah, I mean, Di has something she wants to tell you.'

'Well, Mr Sims, while you were away, quite a few things started to go wrong. Your wife's health scare to start with, and then Liam's injuries.'

'Yeah. Yeah.'

She raised her hand to silence the impending outburst.

'If you will just have a read through this simple contract while I take Leila through to the kitchen and get the coffee underway.'

As the women left him alone in the hallway, he scanned through the two pieces of paper. He put it down, shook his head, and began reading it all over again. When he finally reached the kitchen, all he saw was the radiant face of his Leila. Rushing towards her, he picked her up, twirling her round like a feather. It made him realise how much weight she had lost, but now was not the time to mention it.

'Leila, does this mean … I mean, can we … how has this happened?'

'I take it you approve of the contract Leila and I produced? Now that it's settled, you go and bring the passengers in.'

'You mean, all of them?'

'Yes, they've all had a hand in making this idea grow into fruition, so they should join the celebration of the housewarming.'

Chapter 78

Finally, John got to sit down with Barbara, Kevin, and that mystery file.

'Barbara, it says here that your father raised you until you were three years old, and that your mother died a couple of months after your birth. So, that doesn't really have much to do with Marsh Flats.'

'In some of the other papers there are a lot more details,' said Barbara, rather miffed that John had said what he had without looking at everything.

'Okay, let's start by putting all the dated ones in numerical order, and the others in location order.'

Soon the table was littered with papers of all shapes and sizes. Some white pieces were now very yellowed with age – this is what caught John's eye. As he opened it, he found himself reading quite a private letter from someone called Anne Marie Simmonds to a Mary Simmonds.

'Barbara, what did you say your mother's name was?'

'Mary. Mary Simmonds until she changed it to Stoneman.'

John had been watching Marie's face carefully and he got

the reaction he was hoping for. Firstly, her face paled, then her bottom lip quivered ever so slightly.

'John, is that—? I mean, could it—?'

'Wait a bit, dear. Barbara, do you know your grandparents name by any chance?'

'Um … Oh, yes, Anne Simmonds!'

'Then it is all falling into place—well, sort of. It was you and Kevin speaking of your older brother's friend who wouldn't go to work with all the others at Marsh Flats. The years didn't seem to fit but after reading a couple of these old letters it all makes sense.'

'What do you mean, John? Or are you keeping it a secret all to yourself?'

'Well, take this one letter from Anne Marie to what we now know to be her mother Anne Simmonds.'

I know I was a real disappointment to you and father, but I thought I could right some of that by helping Ronald stage his disappearance so he couldn't be found and charged with the offences he has committed. But now, I find I'm expecting and Tony is the father, but he won't marry me because we're too young. When I've had the baby, I'll put it up for adoption and then return home, if you'll have me, to start a fresh life. I've changed my name also, so the baby will have a fresh start with a new name – Stoneman.

'So, you see, Kevin, that's who your older brother had a crush on – Anne Marie Simmonds, who, like Barbara, had beautiful long red hair.'

Barbara had been very still as she watched her family bloom like a rose. She was fascinated with some things that had already become clear.

'Marie, dear, I know how you feel about looking for skeletons, but if Anne Marie changed her name, do you think perhaps her brother Ronald changed his name also?'

'Why, John? He didn't ever make any contact with the

family again. I can remember how upset they were when Uncle William and Auntie Anne thought their son had died, and it hurt them more when Anne Marie up and left.'

Dylan had not said a word in all the time that the adults were passing papers back and forth. In fact, his grandparents thought he was daydreaming with his book.

'Grandy, if that man changed his name, could it have been just a shorter part of his own name?'

'What do you mean, boy? Oh my lord, I think he's got it. Dylan, do you mean maybe using the first three letters?'

'Yes, Grandy. He could be Mr Ronald Sim.'

'That's close, but I think it was Ronald Sims.'

Now it was Marie's turn to voice her opinions.

'John, does that mean he could be the father of Ronnie Sims?'

'Got it in one!'

'Nana, does that mean Liam is going to find more of his grandparents?'

'It certainly looks that way, doesn't it?'

'I wish they had a phone in that unit that worked. I'd like to ring Liam up to see how he is now he's home.'

At that remark, Barbara began feeling quite uncomfortable.

'Ah … I'm supposed to have already invited you all to a housewarming, but I'm afraid I got too involved in all this. Marie, you know Di Brown's address, don't you?'

'Yes, of course, we'll follow you and Kevin.'

'Aw … Do I have to go, Nana?'

'Sorry, there's no getting out of this invitation. I think you will enjoy yourself.'

'Aw, Nana, at a teacher's place?'

The two cars left together and were soon heading into the wide, leafy streets. Dylan was sitting as close to the door as he possibly could. Marie had never seen her grandson sulk this badly. As John drove into the driveway to make it easier for Dylan, peace was shattered by the voices of many children. Dylan still would not look out of the window. John motioned to Liam to get in the back of the car.

'Grandy, I said I wasn't getting out.'

'Hi Dilly, why ya not gettin' out?'

'Liam, why are you here?'

'Ya won't believe this. This is where Mam, Da, and us live now!'

'You mean, with Mrs Brown?'

'No. Jus' us.'

'Nana, does this mean Liam and I can spend time together here and at home?'

'Well, I think you'll need to speak to Mr and Mrs Sims.'

chapter 79

Di Brown thought she would ease quietly into retirement. That in itself caused her to chuckle to herself. Puss opened his sleepy eyes at the sound.

'Quiet retirement, Puss, that's what I said. Far from it, but I think even you are adapting to the children remarkably well. I saw you the other day riding round the lawn in that old doll's pram.'

The phone rang at that moment.

'Hello, Di Brown.'

'Hi, it's Angie. Are you doing much next Saturday?'

'Well, I know I'm not marking books or preparing lessons.'

'Yes, your class is still functioning, and no I'm not overloading myself, but with the improvement in Dylan's legs and back, I'm beginning to have doubts. What will happen when he finally goes back to his parents? And how are you and the Sims settling in?'

Angie could imagine, through hearing the comments at school from Liam, Suzy and Dylan, that Di was living in clover. She had company, purpose, and a live-in gardener and handy person.

'Well, Angie, the answer is it's nothing to the first question and absolutely wonderfully to the second. What's happening on Saturday?'

'Um … Well … It's, well, it's a double engagement celebration – mine and Barbara's.'

'Well, well. I must say you were both dragging your feet. I'd have thought this would have happened weeks ago.'

'But you know me, Di. I had to be really sure.'

The details were being discussed between them as to where and when.

'One thing I must ask, did you put Leila up to offering help with the catering and, what's more, finding that venue at such a reasonable rate?'

'No. Sorry, I can't take credit for that.'

'Who then? I told Barbara it was sure to be you.'

As they discussed a few other ideas, it suddenly dawned on Angie that she'd heard Liam and Dylan secretly planning something, although she never inquired what it was.

'Di, do you think Leila got the Pacific group to help her in a way of paying back as well as thanking us all?'

'You're probably right there. It's not every day that fairytales come true, you know.'

'Have you met Leila's parents?'

'Yes, they were here the other day for lunch, which went on for hours. Leila is so happy and proud that her father and husband are seeing eye to eye. Ronnie and Mr Tanekaha were even out in the garden discussing some problem Ronnie had run into with aphids, of all things.'

'It sure is strange the way things have unravelled after being tied up and knotted so savagely for all those years.'

'Amen to that, Angie. Amen.'

Chapter 80

'Hello?'

'Hello, may I speak to Eric Brothers?'

'Sorry, he's not in at the moment.'

'Well, Jimmy, I'll speak to Jimmy.'

'Sorry, your luck's not in today. Jimmy's with Brothers. May I take a message?'

'Whom am I speaking to?'

'Sorry, sir, I'm PC Amy Dowd.'

'Could you tell Eric that Bruce Evans rang, and I'll ring again tomorrow at about this time?'

'Yes sir, Mr Evans.'

Bruce didn't even try to let PC Dowd know that he was in fact Detective Superintendent; it wasn't worth the hassle. Later that day, Jimmy returned earlier than expected because he'd gotten a lift from the airport.

'Hi, Jimmy.' Amy beamed as she looked up from the front desk.

'From now on it'll be Sergeant Jimmy, if you please.'

'You did it. You got your third stripe.'

'Yeah. I'll be off now. Just called in to let you know Brothers is coming on the next flight. See you tomorrow, Amy.'

Jimmy headed to the boarding house where he had a room. He waved to the handyman who was changing a blown light bulb.

'G'day there, young Jim.'

'Yeah, g'day to you, too,' Jimmy replied as he kept walking up the staircase.

'Hey, wait up. Your dad dropped in and said to tell you he'd be at Tony Johnson's place for a couple of days.'

'Thanks, Reg. Thanks a heap.'

He plopped himself down on the bed, glad to have taken the weight off his feet for a while. As he lay there, he looked up at the ceiling, watching a fly getting dangerously close to a spider waiting in its web.

Oh, Mama, I wish you were here today to see how your boy has made something of himself. I think you'd be proud. As this thought finished in his head, the curtain twirled around on itself, even though there was not even the slightest breeze outside.

Thank you, Mama, for watching over me. Now I know you really are proud of your son, Jimmy.

About the Author

Andrea was born in Hobart, Tasmania in 1949.

She was known as Nandy during her school days in the nearby suburb of Moonah and enjoyed an uneventful childhood.

Andrea held a variety of clerical assistant positions.

She married and lived on the East Coast of Tasmania, having only one child, Kate.

Andrea now resides in Bundoora, Victoria near her daughter and family, Kate, Tim, and Zoey Ryan.